The War's End

CECELIA SCHMIDT

True joy can only come from
Contentment in Christ!

Cecelia Schmidt

1 Tim. 6:6

Author's Note

The War's End is not meant to be historically accurate. All characters and events are fictitious, and any resemblance to real persons or events, living or dead, is purely coincidental.

Historical Note

Interracial marriage (between whites and blacks) was not legalized in America until 1967.

Dedication

~Above all others, I dedicate this book to my Lord and Savior, Jesus.~

This book is also dedicated to my brother and sister, whom the Lord brought into our lives through adoption. I thank God for making you a part of our family and pray that you will grow up loving and serving Him with your whole heart, mind, soul, and strength. My hope is that through this book, others will see that skin color and bloodline are not the prerequisites to having a true family, but rather hearts knit together by God's loving and sovereign plan. The Lord has placed you in our lives, and I am so thankful for that. I love you both very much.

I'd also like to thank my parents, siblings, and friends for their help, support, and encouragement. I am also grateful for all of the wonderful people I've met at homeschool conventions over the last couple years who encouraged me to write more books. Without all of your kind words and support, I would not have written the second and third book in this series.

Lastly, a special thanks to Mr. Bill Potter for his encouragement and kindness in answering all of my historical questions. You are a tremendous blessing to my family and me, and we thank God for you.

Praise for
The War's End

"*The War's End* is the third and final installment in *The War Rages On* series. Set in the post-reconstruction South, the book concludes the story of David and Grace Carver, telling their struggle with raising Eliza, a black orphaned girl, in a society steeped in prejudice and bigotry. The book explores challenging themes such as children coming to grips with adoption, dealing with bullies, as well as the series' overarching message of redemption from sin. The book does not drag, however, but keeps a lighthearted and entertaining tone. This is perhaps because above all, this book is about joy, the joy found in Christ."

-Jacob, age 19

"This is a very interesting and compelling story of life in the 19th century. It kept our attention with plenty of action, engaging plotlines, and an uplifting message. *The War's End* is a satisfying conclusion to this trilogy. We really enjoyed it!"

-Amelia, age 18, and Addison, age 15

"Like its predecessors, *The War's End* is an incredible installation to Cecelia's series. From the well-executed characters and circumstances, to the meticulous attention to historical accuracy, to the strong Gospel themes that permeate Cecelia's writing style, every aspect of this book is a testament to its author's prodigious abilities."

-Samuel, age 16

"The perfect way to end the series. Cecelia has given us a story that will resonate in the minds of anyone who chooses to pick it up. She teaches us the importance of family while continuing her theme of an inspiring redemption story. Exactly what the teens of today need to hear!"

-Lily, age 14

CONTENTS

CHAPTER ONE

INTRODUCTIONS

Life is unexpected. So often the things we hope and plan for never come to pass, and the things that we'd never ask for are those we receive. Such was the case with David and Grace Carver. They would have never have planned to someday adopt a child, but that is exactly what the Lord had called them to do. If it had been their choice, David and Grace would have never chosen to have their friends Daniel and Elizabeth taken so young, but yet, that is what God had planned for their lives, all for His glory and their good. As David and Grace watched the years unfold, they realized what a truly wonderful plan it was.

In the early years of their marriage, the young couple was unable to have children of their own, and this caused Grace a great amount of grief. When the Lord ordained them to be Eliza's parents, it was unexpected, shocking, and a bit challenging at first for them to accept. When Grace came to the realization, however, that this was a blessing in disguise, she joyfully welcomed Eliza into their home, and they instantly became a family. David and Grace nurtured, provided for, and protected Eliza as if she were their own. They saw no barrier, no difference between them, even though they were white and she was not. They loved her as their own child. This was only possible because of one simple truth: there are ties stronger than blood, and true love is the strongest bond of all. It's the ultimate love that Christ showed when He died on the cross for people of all nationalities and backgrounds. It's the compassionate love that allows a couple to welcome a child of

a different race into their home and call her "family." This was
the love that David and Grace had for Eliza.

However, Eliza was not to be the only family that the
young couple had. Less than three years after David and
Grace adopted, a child was born to them: a beautiful baby girl.
Due to the promise they had made to each other years earlier,
David and Grace named their baby girl Elizabeth, but "Ellie"
quickly became her nickname. Ellie was a stark contrast to
her older sister Eliza. With a round face, blue eyes, and dirty
blonde hair, she could not have looked more different from her
lean-faced, brown-eyed, dark-haired sister. Yet this difference
in appearance did not bother Eliza, who had never known
anyone in her short lifetime but white-skinned people. She
hardly took any notice at all and saw her life as normal.

From the moment she was born, Ellie was Eliza's "ill' sissa",
and Eliza watched out for her as a mama bear watches over
her cubs. Wherever Ellie was, Eliza was right there beside her,
petting her, kissing her, and simply loving on her. The same
can be said for Ellie. Once she could toddle, Ellie followed
Eliza everywhere. "Up 'Liza!" was her favorite thing to say, and
she always wanted to be either on Eliza's lap or in her arms.
Their relationship was impenetrable.

Once baby Daniel came along, things changed even more.
Eliza, though only eight years old, was relied upon to care for
her two younger siblings and help around the house and farm.
Some might say this was too much for a child of her age, but
she bore her duties as the eldest with a smile on her face and
a song in her heart.

Outside of their own cabin, the Carvers also had close ties
with the Koch family. Jonathan and Anna were also parents
to three young children: Aaron, Margaret, and Samuel. Since

the three children were nearly identical in age to the Carver children, they did everything together. From the beginning, it was Aaron and Eliza this, Margaret and Elizabeth that. Then, once Samuel and Daniel began to walk, whenever their families were together, they were inseparable too.

As for the Miller family, their lives were very different from the the Carvers and Kochs. After her husband was hanged for his crimes, Mrs. Miller fell into a state of depression, spending most of her days alone in the lonely silence of her empty cabin. Not more than a year after her husband's death, she suffered a heart attack and died. Her death was relatively unnoticed, except by her daughter, Lillian.

Lillian grew to be a beautiful young woman. At the young age of seventeen, she married a wealthy plantation owner by the name of Henry Wilson, who caringly took her in less than a month after her mother's death. He was a respectable gentleman, tall, dark, and handsome. Henry provided Lillian with a large home, plenty of servants, and everything her heart could desire, except for true joy and contentment. For after the death of her father and mother, Lillian was forever changed. She could be clothed in the finest silks, doused in the sweetest perfumes, and adorned with the most expensive jewelry, but her heart was still empty. There was something she lacked that money could not buy. She loved Henry—as best she could— but she despised herself. In her inmost thoughts, she loathed the day she was born and wished that she could have died right along with her brother and parents. She believed in nothing, except that which she could see, hear, and touch. Her smiling countenance was nothing more than a façade. Inside, her heart was broken and mourning: mourning life and mourning death.

Less than a year after they were married, Lillian gave birth to twins. Strong, healthy boys, the brothers looked nothing alike. Robert, the older one, was tan with dark eyes and dark hair like his father, and James was fair-skinned with freckles, dirty-blonde hair, and blue eyes like his mother. The boys were handsome in appearance, but ugly at heart, for they would grow up to be rebellious fools just like their grandfather had been.

Lillian took great pride in her sons, and their presence somewhat lifted her grief and bitterness. They also bound Lillian and Henry closer together, for they now had a visible sign of their love. The family seemed happy with their privileged life, for the most part, but it was void of any religion or faith.

The Kochs, the Carvers, and the Wilsons all play an important role in each other's lives, for good and for bad. What they don't realize is just how much the LORD is going to connect them to each other, but they are about to find out.

CHAPTER TWO

BIRTHDAY CELEBRATIONS

"Run, Eliza! Run!" Margaret called to her team mate. She and Ellie stood at the base of the tree, watching Aaron sprinting at full speed in hot pursuit of Eliza. Eliza was within ten feet of the tree and safety.

"Come on, Eliza! You're almost there!" Ellie shouted to her sister.

Leaping with all of her might, Eliza landed next to the oak tree and quickly touched its trunk.

"Ha! I'm safe. And you were so sure you were going to get me!" Eliza taunted her wearied opponent.

"Well, I won the other two games," Aaron playfully boasted. "That's got to count for something."

"Yes, but you didn't win this one, and technically, this one counts the most since it was the last game."

"Eliza's right, Aaron. This game *was* worth the most," Margaret agreed.

"Alright, fine. I can't fight it. Good game, girls." Aaron was not only charming but also a good sport when it came to losing. Shaking each girl's hand, he said, "One of these days, I'd like to catch all three of you."

"In your dreams," Eliza said, raising her eyebrows and smiling slyly at Aaron, who did the same.

"Girls! Aaron! Lunch is ready," Grace called.

"Coming!" said the girls while Aaron went to gather Daniel and Samuel. He found them behind the cabin, pretending their small sticks were knights' swords and the tall oak tree a terrible dragon.

"You are no match for me, you foul beast!" Sir Daniel challenged the fire-breathing monster. A blast of fire shot down from the red-skinned dragon's mouth, and the two heroes had to leap out of the way so as not to be consumed by the flames. The leap was not far enough for Sir Daniel, however, and the end of his frayed cape caught ablaze.

"Is that the best you could do?" Sir Daniel taunted, and with a shrill cry, he and Sir Samuel rushed toward the hideous beast, swords extended. The dragon snapped at the courageous knights, who both dodged its deadly jaws. Plunging their swords into the beast's abdomen, the stout-hearted heroes inflicted deadly wounds until their foe lie vanquished.

While glorious, this victory did not solve the other problem still at hand: Sir Daniel's cape was now engulfed in flames, and he could not remove it.

"My cape! It's caught on my armor! I can't get it off!"

Sir Samuel, a fast-thinker, scanned his surroundings. His eyes glanced upon a small creek. Luck was in their favor, for a bucket sat beside the water's edge. As fast as lightning, he scooped up the bucket, filled it with water, then ran back to Sir Daniel, who was now rolling on the ground trying to put out the fire.

"Here!"

Sir Samuel dumped the water on his friend, extinguishing the flames.

At this heroic act, a nearby onlooker, whom the knights had not yet noticed, burst out laughing.

"Well done, Sir Samuel! A most noble gesture."

The heroes quickly awoke from their imaginative mindset,

and became, once again, boys with sticks, one of whom was now sopping wet.

"Aaron!" Samuel shouted at his brother, slightly angered. "Have you been there the whole time?"

"No, but I've been here long enough to see you slay the dragon and extinguish Sir Daniel's flaming cape," Aaron replied with a laugh.

"Why'd you have to spy on us and ruin everything?" Samuel threw his stick down and crossed his arms.

"I wasn't spying. I just came to tell you that lunch is ready, and we have to go in."

"Okay. Okay. We're coming," Samuel replied with a little huff.

Aaron turned and walked back to the cabin, unable to suppress the quiet chuckle that escaped his lips.

Helping up his sopping companion, Samuel sighed, "Brothers," shaking his head.

"It doesn't seem like it'd be *that* bad to have an older brother," Daniel responded.

"Yah, it's not too bad. He's a pretty good brother for the most part, but sometimes I just get tired of him."

The boys strode back to the cabin, feeling slightly humiliated at Aaron having discovered their game, but mostly proud of their brave defeat of the fiery dragon, who had been every bit as real and horrifying in that moment as anything else.

"I don't think my mom's gonna be too happy," Daniel said, staring at his clothes, which were dripping wet.

"I dumped the water on you," Samuel responded. "If she gets angry at you, I'll tell her it was my fault because it was."

Daniel took a deep breath as if to brace himself for the scolding that was sure to come, and the two friends stepped into the cabin.

As soon as Grace turned around, she saw her son, soaking wet.

"Daniel, what on earth happened?" she exclaimed.

"It was my fault, Aunt Grace," Samuel defended. "We were playing knights and dragons." Samuel hung his head, embarrassed that he had to disclose their silly game, "and Daniel's cape caught on fire from the dragon, so I threw a bucket of water on him to put it out."

Grace could not help but smile and held back a giggle that she knew would humiliate the boys.

"Well, it was a noble cause, Samuel," Grace comforted the small boy, "and since it was all in good fun, I'm not upset with either of you. Though, I don't know what we're going to do about your clothes, Daniel. You can't very well sit at the table like this."

"He can borrow a pair of Samuel's clothes," Anna offered.

"What do you say, young man?" Grace asked, looking down at her son.

"Thank you, Aunt Anna."

"You're welcome, Daniel."

Grace led Daniel into the tiny bedroom and helped him change into Samuel's clothes.

"I'm sorry, Mama," Daniel apologized as Grace finished buttoning his shirt.

"What did I tell you? I'm not angry with you. I know you were just having some fun." Grace paused, a smirk crossing her face. "I do have one request," she continued.

"What's that?"

"Next time, try not to let your cape catch on fire."

Daniel chuckled, and so did Grace.

"Yes, ma'am," he replied, wrapping his arms around her neck in a big hug. She snuggled him back and whispered, "I love you, Daniel."

"I love you, too, Mama."

His sweet voice rung in her ears, and it was a moment that was forever etched in her mind.

"Now come on. Let's go eat that delicious lunch, huh?"

"Mmm-mm. I'm starving!"

"I bet you are! Fighting a dragon is hard work."

"Mama!" Daniel pleaded with her to stop her teasing, kind and harmless as it were.

"Alright, I won't say another word about it."

Grace and Daniel joined the merry group in the kitchen where Anna had laid out all the delicious food. The adults sat at the table and the children on the floor in their own little circle.

"I can't believe we're celebrating your birthdays again already," Anna told Aaron and Eliza. "This year has gone by so fast."

"I remember when you two were babies," Grace reminisced. "And now look at you both…fifteen years old!"

"And in just a couple more months, we'll have another birth to celebrate," Anna said joyously, smiling at Grace.

"I wonder if the baby will be a boy or a girl?" Samuel asked, hoping it would be a boy so he and Daniel would have another playmate.

"I hope Mama has a boy so I can have a baby brother to

play knights and wrestle with like Pa does with me," Daniel said.

"Not me," Ellie rebutted. "I'd like a baby sister to dress up and play dolls with."

"What about you, Eliza?" Grace asked her daughter. "Would you like a brother or a sister?"

"I don't really have a preference." She chuckled, knowing that their discussion was not going to control the gender of the baby. "I know we're gonna have fun either way. It's another baby to continue our traditions with."

"That's a good way to look at it, Eliza," David replied.

Since Aaron and Eliza's birthdays were less than a month apart, the Kochs and Carvers had begun a tradition when the two were just toddlers of celebrating them together. Each year, the kids, as well as the adults, looked forward to the celebration.

Eliza was just a baby when her parents, Daniel and Elizabeth, were taken from this life to the next. She did not remember them, nor the tragedy, and recognized herself as being only a member of the Carver family and none other. David and Grace had chosen not to discuss it, for the memory of their dear friends' deaths was a deep wound in their hearts. They saw no benefit in disclosing the painful reality to their daughter.

Eliza felt at home among these people who were not her flesh and blood and did not bear the same skin color. David and Grace were her parents. Ellie and Daniel were her siblings. There was no question of that in her mind. No prejudice existed inside the safe barriers of home. As far as the racial hatred that did exist outside of David and Grace's control, Eliza was shielded from that with the utmost love and protection from her parents.

Schooling Eliza at home was an important part of her being protected from the bigotry of the outside world. Ellie and Daniel, however, attended the little school in town with the Koch children. At times, Eliza wished she could join them, but for the most part, she was content at home with her mother as her teacher and the kitchen table as her desk. Many times after school, friends Aaron, Margaret, and Samuel would accompany Ellie and Daniel back to their cabin to do homework together. Aaron would help the boys with their arithmetic since that was their weakest subject, and Eliza would assist the girls with their spelling and grammar. Afterwards, they would sometimes get a short time to play before the Kochs had to return home. The two families were inseparable and the children best of friends. Aaron and Eliza were particularly close since they were so close in age, which made it even more enjoyable to celebrate their birthdays together each year.

Since hide-n-seek had been the children's favorite game since the time they were young, Aaron, when he was just six years old, had suggested the parents hide their birthday presents so they could look for them. Ever since then, both the Kochs and Carvers had done it every year for all of their children, and this tradition was perhaps the one all the children looked forward to the most.

"When are we gonna do the birthday present hunt?" Samuel asked his father. Everyone had just finished their meal.

"I think now is just a good a time as any," Jonathan responded. "What do you think, dear?"

"Let's do it!"

"I'll get the gifts!" Daniel leapt up and ran to the bedroom where the gifts had been concealed.

"Close your eyes, you two!" Grace told them, even though Aaron and Eliza already knew the rules of the game. They had to keep their eyes closed until their parents and siblings left the cabin. This way, they couldn't even get a hint of what their gifts were by the size, shape, and wrapping.

Eliza and Aaron were both extremely competitive, and this made the game even more thrilling.

"I hope I find my present first this year. I can't let you beat me for the third year in a row," Eliza told Aaron as they sat inside the cabin while their families hid the gifts.

"Yah, that wouldn't look so good, but then again, everyone knows I'm better at hide-n-seek than you," Aaron replied with a smirk.

"Hah!" Eliza scoffed. "Says the one who lost to me less than an hour ago!"

"You know I let you win. If I had been running full speed, I would've caught you within the first three seconds."

"Would not!"

"Would to!"

"Would not!"

"Would to!"

Eliza and Aaron glared at each other for a long moment, until Eliza burst out laughing. Aaron joined right in. Once they calmed down and caught their breath, Aaron whispered, "Would not!" to which Eliza responded with a little backhand to his arm.

"I'm gonna miss this when we get older," Eliza sighed

with a hint of disappointment in her voice. "But I certainly won't miss you beating me."

"There's no place you can hide where I won't be able to find you, Eliza Grace," Aaron replied matter-of-factly. "That's just the simple truth."

"Well," Eliza said, tilting her head, "if it's the truth, I might as well learn to accept it."

"Yup. I guess you should."

Eliza smiled. Aaron felt like more than a friend; he felt like a brother. She could laugh and talk with him just as comfortably as she could with Ellie or Margaret.

"You two, ready?" Anna called. "Come on out."

"You have five minutes to find your gifts," Grace said. "On your mark. Get set. Go!"

Eliza and Aaron dashed off to hunt for their presents. Eliza ran around the cabin, and Aaron raced to the creek. Eliza searched high and low. Aaron searched near and far. Each scanned the grounds, but found no trace of their gifts.

After three minutes passed, they were beginning to get nervous. Time was running out, and each were feeling the pressure of the competition.

"Where on earth did you guys hide these gifts?" Eliza shouted out as she frantically searched behind the rain barrel.

"That's for us to know and you to find out," Grace answered back.

One minute remained. Ellie and Margaret whispered to one another, and Daniel and Samuel chuckled at their siblings' seeming failure.

Let's see, Aaron thought. *I've searched everywhere, and it's nowhere on the ground. So it's got to be…* Aaron looked around until his eyes landed on his birthday gift.

"I found it! I found my gift!" Aaron ran to the cabin where Eliza stood totally perplexed.

"What?!?" she asked in shock. "Where?"

Aaron pointed up at the cabin roof. Sure enough, there was his wrapped gift, just a few inches from the edge.

"Well done, Aaron," Jonathan said, giving his son a slap on the shoulder. "I was pretty confident that neither of you would be able to find them."

"You were right about one of us, at least," Eliza sighed. "I have no idea where mine is."

The parents smirked at one another, and the siblings giggled.

"What is it?" Eliza wondered.

"Samuel, come here," Jonathan called to his son. Lifting him up, he set Samuel on his shoulders. Samuel then reached up and retrieved not one gift from the roof, but two.

"What? My gift was up there, too?" Eliza asked with a smile.

"That's a first," Aaron commented. "Our gifts have never been in the same spot."

"Which is why we did it," Anna replied. "We knew you guys wouldn't expect it."

Eliza and Aaron shook their heads and chuckled.

"Well," Eliza muttered, "I know when I've been beaten. Congratulations, Aaron." Eliza extended her hand, and Aaron received it.

"Technically," Ellie quipped with a grin, "he beat you twice."

"I know, I know," Eliza replied, rolling her eyes.

"In Eliza's defense," Aaron added, striving to be a gentleman once again, "it was the hardest hunt we've had so far."

"Good," David answered. "That was the point."

Everyone let out a laugh, except for Daniel, who was growing slightly impatient.

"Can you guys *please* open your gifts now? I'm dying to know what they are!" he pleaded.

Aaron and Eliza carefully opened their packages, unlike their younger siblings, who usually tore into the wrapping, paying no mind to how delicate the gift might be.

"My own razor!" Aaron exclaimed. He turned it over, examining the craftsmanship.

"That's the one you wanted, isn't it?" Anna asked her son.

"Yes! Thank you so much!" Aaron gave his parents a huge hug.

"Now you can finally get rid of that beard of yours," Eliza joked, shooting a sly glance at Aaron, who had almost no facial hair.

"She's always teasing me for wanting a razor," Aaron told his parents. "Well, pretty soon I *will* have a beard, Eliza, and I'll let it grow real long. Then you won't be able to tease me anymore."

"Yah, sure you will," Eliza said sarcastically.

If this discussion had been between any of the other siblings, it might have turned into an argument. Because it was Eliza and Aaron, however, it remained playful. All of the teasing and antagonizing was just innocent fun. In all the years they'd known each other, they'd never argued, not even once.

"Ribbons!" Eliza cheered. "They're beautiful!"

Beaming from ear to ear, Eliza pulled three from the package. They were her favorite colors: pink, light blue, and purple.

"I want to try one on." Eliza took the pink ribbon and tied it in her hair.

"I love it!"

"I'll take the blue one," Aaron teased. "It would complement my blue eyes just perfectly."

"Oh, be quiet you!" Jonathan rustled his son's hair.

Eliza glanced back down at the wrapping to find yet another gift. "A handkerchief! Thank you so much!"

She wrapped her arms around her mother, who tenderly kissed her forehead.

"You're welcome, Eliza."

Eliza stroed the lovely piece of fabric and gazed at her new treasures.

"You're it!" Daniel tagged Aaron, anxious to play another game. Aaron caught up to him in no time, and the girls decided to join in the fun.

Surely, life couldn't get any better than this.

CHAPTER THREE

DIFFERENT WORLDS

Smoke rose from the dying embers of the crackling campfire. Its noise echoed in the stillness of the woods. Only the occasional hooting of an owl could be heard. Two horses stood a short ways off, grazing. Their owners warmed themselves by the fire, each in complete silence. Their appearances conveyed that they had stumbled across hard times.

The older of the two slouched against an old log, his arms folded across his chest with his wide-brimmed hat tipped slightly over his eyes. His coat was one button short and his leather boots had seen better days. His shoulder-length, dirty blonde hair was pulled back loosely in a ponytail, and a short beard completed his disheveled yet handsome appearance.

Though both brothers had becoming features, the younger was definitely the more attractive of the two. His clothes were not quite as worn, and his hair shorter and neatly kept. His big, brown eyes and clean-shaven face presented a more innocent countenance. Unlike his brother, he was restless and paced for several minutes until his brother's silence compelled him to speak.

"Jake, I can't keep doing this anymore! I'm through. You hear me? I'm through!"

"Oh, quit your rambling, Max! You get like this whenever you're nervous. Just sit down and cool off. Besides, I'm older and you'll do as I say," he replied nonchalantly, not moving from his slouched position.

Max, though a bit impulsive at times, always yielded to

his brother's authority in the end. It was Jake who had talked him into running away from home with him when they were just boys, and it was Jake who had led them into their lives of crime. Max loved his brother, but lately he had grown agitated of his demanding and controlling attitude. For years, he had stuck by Jake's side, even when it meant serving ten years in prison. For all of Max's loyalty, however, Jake never once showed any signs of gratitude.

"What are we gonna do, Jake?" Max muttered nervously. "We just got out of prison, and already we've messed things up. I can't spend the rest of my life being a hunted man! Next time, it won't be ten years, Jake. We'll be in for good."

At this, Jake sat up quickly, and in a fury, he shouted, "Don't you think I know that? If you'd just keep quiet for a minute, maybe I'd be able to hear myself think!"

Jake glared at his brother, then pulled a cigar from his coat pocket. Striking a match on the bottom of his boot, he lit the cigar and tossed the match into the fire. Letting out a long puff of smoke, he said, "We'll work our way east. A change of scenery would do us both some good."

"That suits me fine."

"Well, even if it didn't, that's what we'd be doing!" Jake snarled, uninterested in any of his brother's thoughts or feelings.

Max sat down next to his brother, resting his head against the log.

"You know," Max added with a warm smile, "I wouldn't mind a nice, quiet place in the country with a pretty, little wife to come home to every day, homemade meals, two, maybe three kids. It's times like these, Jake, when I...well I wish we hadn't…" Max stopped mid-sentence when he caught Jake's cold stare.

"Wake up, Max. That ain't the life we've got."

"I know," Max mumbled, letting out a long, dejected sigh. "Believe me, I know."

*   *   *

Lillian and Henry Wilson sat on the couch in their living room. A glowing fire radiated its beams from the fireplace. Their sons' elderly tutor, Mr. Davis, sat across from them. Their countenances were solemn, for it was unusual that Mr. Davis should require a private audience with them.

"I'm sorry, but I just can't tutor your boys any longer." Mr. Davis's voice stressed frustration and exhaustion.

A look of shock swept across Lillian's face. What could Mr. Davis possibly have against her boys?

"Why?" was her curt reply.

"Well, I—I just can't handle them, Mrs. Wilson. They spend most of their time goofing off and playing nasty tricks. Why, just the other day, they poured ink all over my papers, and refused to own up to their wrongdoings. And, now, they've gotten to the point where they refuse to do their work all together. I'm not the one to tell you both how to raise your children, but—" Mr. Davis stopped to adjust the spectacles on his nose.

"What do you suggest, Mr. Davis?" Henry asked, interested in the scholarly man's opinion.

After a short delay, Mr. Davis responded, "I suggest you send them to school."

"Send them to school?" Lillian almost shouted. "My boys in a public schoolhouse? With commoners' children?"

"And why not, Mrs. Wilson? It would do your boys a world of good to learn to sit quietly in a classroom, wait to speak until they're spoken to, and obey the directions given them without hesitation. Until their behavior proves differently, they don't *deserve* to have a private tutor."

"I think we will be the judge of that," Lillian snapped back. "We know what is best for our boys."

Mr. Davis lowered his voice and leaned forward to add emphasis to his words.

"Some good, old-fashioned discipline is what is best for your boys, Mrs. Wilson," he stated. Then, smiling gently and tipping his hat, he offered them a "Good evening," picked up his briefcase, and left.

"Well, I never!" Lillian gasped after he was gone. "I can't believe you sat there and did nothing! You just let him insult our sons…and us!"

"He's right, dear," Henry spoke softly to his irritated wife. "Our boys should learn what it's like to have to go to school and cooperate with other children."

"But our boys aren't like those other children, Henry. They're—"

"Spoiled," he stated plainly. Seeing Lillian's eyes bulge at this statement, he sighed and calmly invited her to sit beside him, for she was currently pacing back and forth, venting her frustration.

"Lillian," he gently took her hands in his. "It's time you be honest with yourself."

When Lillian opened her mouth to protest, Henry quickly

added, "Let me finish. Never once in their life have Robert and James ever stepped foot in a schoolhouse. Mr. Davis is right: it *would* be good for them to see how other children are educated. He's also right when he says that our boys lack discipline. Now we both know that for the past fourteen years I have been trying to teach those boys to respect authority and behave appropriately. But I have been unable to do that... because of you. If you had let me discipline our boys as I saw fit, they wouldn't be in the state that they are in now. If I had done the things they do as a child, my father would have lashed me to the point where I wouldn't have been able to sit for a week."

"Henry! You're not suggesting...you wouldn't dare strike our boys!"

"If they don't stop behaving this way, I'll have no other choice. You have to stop focusing on your feelings and focus more on what's truly best for Robert and James."

"But they...we just..." Lillian stopped when she found her argument unjustified.

"Growing up to be unruly citizens and lawbreakers is *not* what's best for them, Lillian."

Lillian stopped as she came to the realization that her husband spoke the truth.

"You're right, Henry. So what do we do?"

"We put them in school and don't let them get away with *anything*. No disrespect, no disobedience, nothing. Hopefully, if we're consistent, we can undo the damage we've done these past fourteen years. But," Henry paused, looking his wife square in the eyes. "We have to work together on this. I need you on my side, Lillian...for all of our sakes."

*   *   *

Eliza lay in bed, contemplating how wonderful her birthday had been. Not only had they had a party the week before with the Kochs, but today, on her actual birthday, her grandma and grandpa had come over to have a celebration all their own. While she lay there, the door quietly creaked open, and Grace sat down on the bed beside her.

"Did you have a fun birthday, Eliza?" she asked sweetly.

"Yes, Mama. I think this was my favorite birthday yet."

Both mother and daughter spoke in hushed tones so as not to wake Ellie, who slept in the bed beside Eliza.

"I'm glad. You mean the world to your father and me." Bending down to kiss Eliza's cheek, Grace wrapped her arms around her daughter and whispered, "I love you so much."

"I love you, too, Mama," Eliza replied, wrapping both arms around her mother.

"Now you get some sleep and remember to say your prayers."

"I will."

Grace blew a kiss to her daughter and silently shut the door. As soon as she did, Eliza closed her eyes and prayed.

Thank you for my family, Lord. Thank you for Mama, Father, Ellie, and Daniel. Thank you for Grandma and Grandpa. Thank you for the Kochs. Thank you for my birthday, too, and all the great presents. Thank you for loving and watching over me. Amen.

CHAPTER FOUR

BULLIES AND OUTLAWS

School was considered a chore by some of the children who attended, but others with a more positive attitude viewed it as an opportunity to grow and hone their skills. This was the outlook the Carver and Koch children had, and not surprisingly, they were the most well-behaved children there. Though they were not always thrilled to sometimes have to sacrifice their playtime for homework, they did their work with little to no complaints and obeyed their teacher, Miss Barton, without hesitation.

Other students were not as obedient and would find themselves standing in the corner or detained after school, like the Wilson Brothers. Although they were slightly better behaved with Miss Barton than they had been with their tutor, Mr. Davis, it was only the fear of public humiliation that kept them out of major crises. For the most part, they left the other children alone, except for a few spitballs here and there and a shove or two of one of the smaller kids. Besides Aaron, they were the oldest kids in school. Their size alone caused the other children to fear them and overlook any "mishaps" that might occur.

Lunch was one of their favorite times to play pranks, and they found themselves, more than once, having to sit out of recess because of them.

"Give it back!"

"Awwww, you want it? Then come and get it!"

Robert and James threw the boy's sandwich back and

forth over his head. Timmy was one of the little boys and was unable to defend himself against the bullies.

"Come on guys," his high-pitched voice pleaded. "It's not funny!"

"Sure it is!" James laughed.

"Aren't you having fun, Timmy?" Robert mocked as he threw the sandwich back to James.

The small boy was getting frustrated and was on the verge of crying when someone intervened.

"Hey!" James shouted angrily as his pass was intercepted.

"Here you go, Timmy." The hero handed the sandwich back to its owner. "Why don't you go sit with Daniel and Samuel?"

"Okay," Timmy whimpered.

"Hey," the boy gently whispered, bending down to the look the lad in the eyes, "don't let them get to you. They're just bullies. Keep a stiff upper lip."

Timmy nodded and managed to smile through his watery eyes.

"Thanks, Aaron," he said.

Aaron smiled to himself as he watched Timmy join Daniel and Samuel, who gladly welcomed him into their company.

"What do you think you're doing, Koch?" Robert sneered.

"Yah, why'd you have to ruin our fun?" James added.

"Your fun should not come at the expense of Timmy's humiliation," Aaron boldly shot back.

"You can't tell us what to do!" Robert hissed in Aaron's face.

Robert stood eye to eye with Aaron, who was just about an inch taller.

"You're right. I don't," Aaron responded. "But Miss Barton does."

"Tattletale," James mocked.

"You really gonna go snitch to Miss Barton?" Robert sassed.

"I will if you two keep picking on little boys half your size. Miss Barton doesn't like reports like that."

Robert held his head up as he nodded to James and said, "Come on, James. Let's go."

Aaron was left by himself as the two bullies walked away to eat their lunch, making all sorts of nasty faces and comments behind Aaron's back.

Margaret and Ellie had been watching the whole thing unfold from a distance. When it was clear, they walked over to Aaron.

"You did the right thing, Aaron," Margaret commended her brother. "Timmy wouldn't have stood a chance against those bullies."

"Do you think they'll do it again?" Ellie asked.

Aaron sighed, running his fingers through his hair.

"I don't think they'll mess with Timmy again, but they always have a fight to pick with someone."

"Bullies are cowards." Margaret rolled her eyes. "With you here to stand up to them, they probably won't try anything else."

"I wouldn't be too sure," Ellie countered. "Those boys are nothing but trouble. I wish they'd leave our school."

"If they keep this up," Aaron said, "they won't have a choice."

*   *   *

Horses' hooves pounded into the soft dirt as a hot chase ensued. The outlaws were outnumbered two to one, but their horses were fresher, giving them the advantage. Bullets whizzed through the air as the lawmen shot at the outlaws and the outlaws shot back. These outlaws had more riding and shooting experience than the lawmen themselves.

The outlaws pressed their horses to go faster with one hand and shot their pistols with the other. They were doing pretty well until the one went to fire another shot.

"Jake! I'm out!" Max shouted as he dodged an oncoming bullet. "We gotta think of something and fast!"

Jake ignored his brother.

"Come on!" he kicked his horse and fired another shot at the lawmen.

Max's heart was beating rapidly.

We're done for sure! No bullets left, and nowhere to hide. The only chance we got is…

Max breathed heavily as he spotted something small moving in the distance. This was their chance!

"Jake, the train! The train!" Max yelled, frantically hoping, almost praying, that this would be their way out.

Sure enough, there was a freight train chugging at full speed a good ways off from the party. It was coming at them from the right, puffing its black smoke.

"Veer right!" Jake commanded his brother as they pulled their horses' reigns in that direction.

It was nonstop chaos as the lawmen continually fired their guns, and the brothers continually dodged their bullets.

They were approaching the train, and the train was rapidly approaching them. Spotting the men on horseback, the conductor sounded the whistle to warn them. The frenzied outlaws paid no heed. The train was riding too fast to stop. The brothers raced across the tracks just feet in front of the advancing train. Seeing the lawmen approaching and fast, the conductor put on the brakes.

Jake and Max wasted no time. The train was blocking them from the lawmen's view. They yanked their horses to the right and into the thickets, straying from the course the lawmen would have expected them to take. There they waited in silence and suspense.

Shortly after, the lawmen rode across the tracks just as the train came to a halt. Angrily, the conductor shouted, "What's the matter with you, you lunatics? You're gonna wind up dead if you keep riding in front of moving trains like that! If I hadn't stopped—" the conductor gave up trying to reason with the lawmen when he realized his words were to no avail. Riding on at full speed, the lawmen pursued the outlaws, paying no heed to the elderly man's protests.

"Ugh," the conductor muttered in disgust as he sounded the train's whistle, as if to give one last protest to the disappearing lawmen.

Jake and Max waited until the train had gotten a good ways down the tracks before they came out of hiding.

"Phew," Max sighed. "I think we lost 'em." He took his hanky out of his pocket to wipe the sweat dripping from his face.

"That was close…too close. Come on! We're getting out of here." Jake pulled the reigns to the left while scanning to the right for any signs of the lawmen.

"Where are we going now?"

Jake looked his brother square in the eyes.

"Home," he whispered, and Max wondered if Jake was finally longing for a new life, a life of peace?

CHAPTER FIVE

ALL ALONE

The Koch and Carver children sat comfortably together next to the roaring fire. As usual, the older children were assisting the younger ones with their homework while simultaneously attempting to finish their own. Daniel tapped his pencil against the wood floor in frustration.

"I give up!" he huffed after trying to solve the same math problem for the third time. Aaron had walked him through the steps, and even though it was just simple subtraction of three digit numbers, Daniel couldn't seem to grasp the concept. "This problem is just impossible! Why do I have to learn all this stuff anyways?"

"It's all part of expanding your knowledge, Daniel," Grace calmly replied, tapping her spoon on the side of the pot of stew she was preparing. She set it down on the spoon rest and walked over to her struggling son.

"Once you understand these math problems, you'll have a good foundation for learning how to do the harder ones, like the ones Aaron and Eliza do," Grace said, bending down to examine her son's pad of paper.

"But I don't want to learn how to do *harder* ones!" he whined. "These subtraction problems are hard enough!"

"Well, sometimes we have to do things in life whether we'd like to or not, Daniel. It sure is easier if we have a good attitude and don't complain. Now look…" Grace picked up her son's abandoned pencil and worked out the problem on the paper. Daniel's eyes lit up when he saw that it really was solvable.

"Hey!" he exclaimed with boyish delight.

"It really wasn't all that hard, now was it?" Grace said, kissing Daniel's forehead.

"No. It actually looked easy. I want to try the next one." Daniel took the pad and pencil from his mother and began to solve the next problem. This time, he got it right.

"I did it!" he proclaimed proudly.

"You see? It's all about attitude, Daniel. You couldn't solve the first problem because you were too focused on not *wanting* to solve it. When you had a good attitude, though, it made solving the next problem a whole lot easier, didn't it?"

"It sure did!"

"Attitude is everything, Daniel. The way you *think* greatly affects the way you *behave*," Grace told her son, brushing a strand of loose hair out of his face. "If you can learn that lesson just by doing some simple math problems, it will help you a lot when you have to face some tougher challenges later in life."

Daniel leaned up and kissed his mother on the cheek, and Grace stood to finish preparing supper.

Eliza smiled. It was just like her mother to turn everyday things into spiritual lessons.

Attitude is everything, she thought. *The way you think affects the way you behave.*

Eliza continued her work, unaware of the many challenges she would soon face and how significantly this simple truth would change her life.

*   *   *

Jake and Max rode on for hours until the sun had completely set, and they made camp under the stars. The lawmen were long gone, and they were out of harm's way.

While they had been riding, Jake was too concerned with escaping the lawmen to notice the bloody wound on his left arm. One of the bullets had grazed his skin, but it had left a gash several inches long. The bottom part of his sleeve was soaked with blood, and now that there were no more distractions to keep his mind occupied, it became excruciatingly painful.

Max, unlike Jake, still had remnants of a kind heart left in him, and he genuinely cared for his brother's well-being. Noticing his brother's discomfort, he ripped off a long strip of his shirt and went to wrap Jake's arm.

Grabbing his flask, Max poured some of his whiskey, which was almost gone, over his brother's wound.

As Jake grunted in pain, he grumbled, "That hurts!" and shoved Max's hand away.

"You've got to clean it, Jake. It'll get infected," Max gently cautioned.

"Give me that," he mumbled, and snatched the strip of fabric out of Max's hand. Jake struggled to wrap his arm, and when Max offered to help him, Jake responded with a rough, "I can do it myself!"

Max sat down across from his brother and waited a moment to speak.

"Jake, I've been wondering something: Why do you want to go back home? I mean, there's nothing for us there," Max queried.

"That's what you think…aaaaaah!" Jake screamed as he finally managed to tie the bandage around his wounded arm.

"Here's what I've been thinking," he continued, leaning in closer. "We left, what…twenty-two…twenty-three years ago? The old bags are certainly dead by now, and that means dear, baby brother Henry will have taken over the plantation. We'll play it safe: we'll apologize for leaving home, tell him we want to set things straight, and take two jobs in town."

"Now hold on there, Jake!" Max interrupted. "I just said I wanted a change of scenery. I never said I wanted to go home, humiliate myself by apologizing for something I did twenty-some years ago, and then start working a crummy job!"

"Would you just let me finish? We'll keep that act up for a couple months. This way, we'll have earned our reputation back. No one will suspect anything."

"What are you getting at, Jake?" Max's eyebrows furrowed in suspicion.

"Henry will have a little accident, you see? And who will get the plantation then?" Jake asked with a sly grin.

"We will," Max answered, glowing with satisfaction. However, that glow quickly dimmed when Max pondered their plan.

"Wait a second, Jake. What if we get caught?"

"We won't get caught. You have my word on that. Believe me, I'll die before I go back to prison!"

Jake's eyes were filled with hate and revenge. Exhaling a large puff of smoke from his cigar, he maliciously, yet quietly, fumed, "We'll get our revenge, Max. We'll set things straight. After Henry's gone, we'll have everything we ever wanted: a big house, lots of money, servants at our beck and call, maybe a wife, and even some children."

"That would suit me fine."

Max chuckled, reminiscing back to the days when he was a boy, attending school and doing everything imaginable to get a certain young girl's attention.

"You remember Katelyn Barton?" he asked as a wistful mist fogged his eyes.

"Oh brother." Jake sat up straighter, starting to laugh. "You were head over heels in love with her. Remember the time you wrote that love note to her?"

"How could I forget it? It was during math class, and Miss Campbell caught me and made me read it out loud to the entire class."

Jake let out an enormous belly laugh, and Max was surprised to see his brother in such an agreeable mood. For the first time in years, they were having a genuinely good time, laughing and talking about…home. It was this that made Max realize that the place they had both run from so many years ago was the same place that they now longed for the most. The place they had once hated was the one filled with their most precious memories.

"I came this close to proposing to her, Jake," Max agonized. "I wonder if she ever—I'd love to…" Max forgot his sentence as he daydreamed about the life he could have had, the life he wished for now more than anything.

"No point in hoping for anything, Max," came Jake's stern voice, stirring Max from his peaceful thoughts. "That was ages ago. Besides," he chuckled, "she was too good for the likes of you anyways."

Any hope Max had for a better life was suddenly trampled by that one cold statement. Katelyn was the only girl Max had ever loved. If for nothing else, he wanted to go home just to see her. But he had messed up too badly. Surely, he had lost his only chance to win her heart.

As Max lay there under the stars, he felt something he had never felt before. He looked up into the endless expanse of stars and was overwhelmed with loneliness. All the places he and Jake had seen, all the money they had stolen, could not fill that hole in his heart. Money could not buy back all those wasted years. He had left the only girl he had ever loved for the sake of his foolish pride and selfishness. Now, he regretted it, and it was too late. Jake didn't understand. He didn't care about anything or anyone except himself. Max was truly all alone…and it had never hurt as much as it did now. For the first time, he was beginning to feel the terrible weight of guilt from all of his horrible choices.

CHAPTER SIX

SCHOOL TROUBLE

Winter faded away. Blossoming trees and singing birds announced spring's arrival. It was a time of new growth and new life. Grace's fourth child was due in just about a month, and everyone was eagerly anticipating the arrival.

With the end of the school year only a couple months away, some of the children were becoming antsy. With the weather growing warmer, they longed to be outside in the fresh air. Needless to say, a few did not contain their energy very well and took some of their restlessness and frustration out on others. More fights occurred and there was more disrespect in the classroom. The Carver and Koch children were the only ones that could be counted on for respect, obedience, and diligence in their work. When they were annoyed and wished for freedom, they controlled themselves and kept whatever negative feelings they had to themselves. It was very surprising then, when one day, they were involved in a horrible fight.

Margaret and Ellie were playfully riding the see-saw, just a simple plank of wood balancing on an old tree stump, when who should enter the picture but Robert and James. The boys had decided that they wanted the see-saw all to themselves and couldn't have cared less that it was currently occupied. They strutted right over to the girls. James positioned himself right behind Margaret, and Robert jumped on top of the stump.

"What do you think you're doing?" Ellie questioned with a tone of disgust.

"I think it's pretty obvious," Robert sassed back. "We wanna ride the see-saw now."

"We're gonna finish our turn first," Margaret firmly responded as she gave a small push with her feet to get the see-saw going again. James quickly pulled it back down, chuckling in fiendish delight.

"Ah, ah, ah," he reprimanded, "I think you missed our point."

"No, I think it's *you* who missed *our* point: we were here first, and we're going to finish our turn," Ellie said.

The girls weren't budging.

"Apparently you don't know what it means to respect your elders." Robert grinned antagonistically.

"You're not my elder, and I don't have to listen to you," Ellie stated.

Robert's contented grin was replaced with a menacing scowl. In his mind, he was boss, and his blood boiled when anyone told him differently.

"Fine," he sneered. "Have it your way."

"You should have gotten off when you had the chance," James said as he grabbed Ellie's arm and pulled her off the see-saw to the ground. Her left elbow hit hard, and she let out a small cry.

"Ellie!" Margaret yelled and ran over to her friend.

"Maybe next time you'll get off when we tell you," Robert said, feeling quite satisfied with himself as he took his seat on the see-saw.

"Are you alright?" Margaret worriedly asked, helping her friend up.

"Yah, I'm fine. My elbow's just a little sore." Ellie tried to move it, but a pain shot up her arm as she did.

"What happened?" Aaron asked as he ran over with Daniel and Samuel, all having heard Ellie's cry.

"We were riding the see-saw, and Robert and James wanted to get on. They told us to get off, and when we told them that we were gonna finish our turn first, James pulled Ellie right off," Margaret recounted.

"He laid his hands on you?!?" Aaron's tone rose as he immediately grew defensive.

Boldly, he approached the see-saw where the two bullies were chuckling with delight at their victory.

"Get off the see-saw! Now!" he ordered, having no patience for the trouble makers.

"Somebody ain't too happy, James," Robert said, forming a pouty face to mock Aaron.

"You bullied my sister and laid hands on Ellie."

"Now hold on there! I don't want to be accused of bullying nobody," Robert faked innocence. "All we did was ask them to get off the see-saw, and when they wouldn't, James just gave Ellie a little help."

Aaron wasn't falling for their lies.

"Pulling a girl so hard that she hits the ground is not giving her 'a little help.' Now either you get off, or I'll make you get off!"

The see-saw came to a halt as Robert and James approached Aaron. Their arms were crossed in indignation and their faces displayed disgust.

"I thought you were Mr. Peacemaker, Aaron," Robert mocked. "You wouldn't go pickin' a fight, now would ya'? Plus," he smirked, "it was all in good fun."

Aaron had had enough, and he meant business.

"Then so is this!" he declared and punched Robert right in the nose. Robert yelled and fell to the ground. Almost instantly, James then attacked Aaron, and the two were quickly on the ground, engaged in an intense fight. Once he had regained his senses, Robert jumped in. The two were on top of Aaron, and they would have won, had it not been for two brave, little heroes that came running in to help.

"Get off of my brother!" Samuel shouted as he jumped on top of James, wrapped his arms around his neck, and yanked him backwards. Surprisingly, this worked, and James fell backward just as Daniel and Samuel jumped on top of him, swinging punches. This left Aaron and Robert rolling on the ground in an intense wrestling match.

A crowd quickly gathered, and all the schoolchildren had formed a circle around them yelling excitedly. Some were cheering on Aaron to win and others were laughing at the hilarious sight of Daniel and Samuel pinning James to the ground.

The noise drew Miss Barton out of the schoolhouse, and when she saw the boys fighting, she rushed over.

"Boys! Boys!" she yelled, clapping her hands to get their attention. "That's enough!"

Samuel and Daniel got off of James, but Robert and Aaron were still going at it.

"I said, 'That's enough!'" Separating the boys as best she could, Miss Barton dragged both of them to their feet.

"Now," she said, brushing off her skirt, "what is going on here?"

"Aaron wanted to get on the see-saw," Robert lied, "so

he pushed James off. When I came over to try to solve the issue peacefully, he punched me right in the nose for no good reason!"

Lying came so naturally to Robert that anyone who hadn't known him would have thought he was telling the truth. Fortunately for Aaron, everyone present, including Miss Barton, knew he was lying, and Margaret quickly came to her brother's defense.

"That's not true, you liar!" she protested and told Miss Barton the whole story.

Miss Barton let out a huff in frustration and put her hands on her hips.

"I must say I'm very disappointed in you boys. Bullying is not allowed! You are to treat your schoolmates with respect, especially the girls," she firmly stated, casting a hard look of disapproval at Robert and James. "And Aaron, whereas your intentions were right in defending Margaret and Ellie, you should not have punched Robert. You know better than that young man."

"Yes, ma'am," Aaron respectfully answered.

"You realize I'm going to have to punish you all for this sinful behavior?"

Aaron, Samuel, and Daniel nodded while Robert and James just stood there with indignant looks on their faces.

"Go inside, boys, and we'll discuss your punishment. The rest of you have five more minutes of recess, and I suggest you use it wisely," Miss Barton said.

As the boys trudged up the schoolhouse steps to discover their fate, Aaron felt ashamed. While he had defended Margaret and Elizabeth, he had acted in anger and disobeyed

Miss Barton. This had been his first fight at school, and he decided right then and there that as much as it depended on him, he would never get involved in another.

Miss Barton sent the boys home with notes to their mothers, describing what happened and how the boys had been punished. Needless to say, Robert and James' punishment was more severe, but it did nothing to alter their behavior nor give them the desire to act better. They threw the note away before they reached home and made up a horrible lie. When Lillian questioned Robert about his black eye and James about his torn clothes, the boys were quick to blame the whole thing on Aaron and the little ones, leaving Lillian to believe that her boys had been assaulted without cause. Furious, Lillian rode over to the schoolhouse to have a word with Miss Barton.

In the Carver and Koch households, the mothers questioned their children about their disheveled appearances, and the boys gave their mother the notes. Whereas Grace and Anna were both upset with their boys for fighting, they were angrier with Robert and James for instigating it by bullying their girls. Grace was especially furious with James for laying his hands on Ellie, and both moms decided to have their own talk with Miss Barton. They, too, rode over to the schoolhouse to discuss things and arrived shortly before Lillian.

"Well, isn't this a surprise?" Lillian asked upon entering the schoolhouse, finding Grace and Anna already talking with Miss Barton.

"Yes, it is," Miss Barton responded with an annoyed sigh, rolling her eyes. The women all knew that in Lillian's mind her boys were angels, and anyone who tried to say otherwise hardly ever won the argument.

"I suppose we're all here for the same reason," Lillian assumed.

"Yes, I suppose we are, Lillian," Grace answered. "As I was saying, Katelyn," Grace addressed Miss Barton, "I just can't have my children getting hurt at school. I know you've done your best with the Wilson boys, but I—"

"My boys?!?" Lillian exclaimed. With her hands on her hips, she declared, "My boys are not the problem here! It was your boys who attacked first," she shouted, pointing her finger at Anna, "merely out of frustration at not getting their way!"

"Attacked?" Anna questioned. "What are you talking about Lillian?"

"As if you don't know!"

"No, I don't," Anna raised her voice.

"Ladies, please!" Miss Barton exclaimed anxiously. Taking a deep breath, she turned to Lillian and asked, "Did your boys give you a note from me?"

"No, why?" Lillian answered sassily.

"I sent a note home with your boys explaining what happened today and—"

"They told me what happened. It's clear that—"

"Please, Lillian! Let me finish. Now, it's clear to me that you did not hear the true story. Margaret and Ellie were riding the see-saw, and your boys started bullying them because they wanted to ride. When the girls didn't get off, James laid hands on Ellie, injuring her arm in the process. When Aaron stood up for the girls, that's when the fight started. Aaron did swing the first punch, but it was merely out of defense for Margaret and Ellie. Aaron and the Carver boys took responsibility for their actions, but your boys refused to apologize and wouldn't listen to anything I had to say."

There was a long pause as Lillian blushed in embarrassment. She tried to maintain her pride, but it was clear to everyone present that she was sorely upset.

"If I had known, I would have—" Lillian paused, deciding not to finish her sentence. "It still doesn't change the fact that Aaron started the fight."

"You're right, it doesn't," Miss Barton consented. "However, his intentions were right in defending the girls. Your boys had no excuse for bullying."

"They're just children. They make mistakes," Lillian tried in vain to defend her boys once again.

"Blatant disobedience of school rules is not a mistake, Lillian!" Miss Barton was losing her patience. "I've tried my best to contain myself up to this point, but your impertinence compels me to say this: Robert and James have been nothing but trouble ever since they started coming to school, and now they've gone so far as to bully the girls, too. Unless their behavior improves, I'll have no choice but to expel them."

At those words, Lillian's jaw dropped, and she felt seriously offended.

"But you—you can't—" she stuttered. "You can't do that! Their tutor, he—he left and—oh, please!" Lillian became desperate. She didn't know what she'd do if her boys got kicked out of school. "They'll do better. I promise they'll do better!"

A silence ensued as the three ladies actually felt a hint of pity for Lillian, who defended her boys with everything in her yet endured the humiliation and disgrace for their deeds the most.

"With summer only being a few months away," Grace

spoke quietly, "I'd hate to remove my children without first waiting to see if things improve. If there's no change, Ellie and Daniel will not be returning in the fall."

"Neither will my children," Anna added gently. "I just can't have them put in danger."

"Things will change, ladies," Miss Barton sighed. "One way or another, they will change. You'll talk to your boys, Lillian?"

Regaining her composure and pride, Lillian mumbled, "Yes," without looking Miss Barton in the eyes.

Miss Barton nodded and put her hand up to her perspiring brow.

"Hopefully, we'll never have to discuss anything like this again," she appealed, frustrated.

"I hope not," Grace said. "Thank you for your time, Katelyn. Good afternoon, Lillian."

Lillian did not respond to Grace, nor did she say anything to Miss Barton. With her head held high, she strode out of the schoolhouse, huffing in disgust on her way.

That evening, Lillian explained everything that had happened to Henry, who was more than a little upset with his boys' behavior. Lillian could not decide which made her more unhappy: the humiliation she had experienced in the schoolhouse or her boys fighting and lying to her about it. Henry, however, was furious when he found out that Robert and James had been misbehaving for months now and had just been putting on a front at home. He decided to act upon his word and gave Robert and James each a lashing, despite Lillian's protest. On top of that, he took away all their free time for the week and assigned them extra chores to do instead.

After sending the boys to bed with no supper, Henry collapsed on the sofa, resting his head on his hand and exhaling deeply.

"I'm sorry that that upset you, Lillian," he told his wife, who refused to acknowledge him. "But those boys have got to learn that disobedience and bullying are not allowed…here or anywhere else."

"I just can't believe—" Lillian bit her lower lip as she refrained herself from scolding her husband. Despite their differing views on some issues, especially when it came to their boys, she loved Henry and respected him, for the most part. She turned her focus back to the shame she had experienced earlier on. "I can't believe that Robert and James lied to me. I made a complete spectacle of myself at the schoolhouse. I have never been more humiliated in all my life! And of all the people, it had to be in front of Grace and Anna!" she exclaimed, throwing her hands up in the air. "What's worse is Miss Barton actually took their side!"

"And why shouldn't she have?" Henry asked, perplexed. "Our boys were the ones who started it with their bullying. It only makes sense that they were upset. After all, they shouldn't have to worry about their children's safety at school!"

"Safety? Please! If the Carvers were really concerned about their children's safety, they wouldn't have adopted that little Negro girl after her parents were murdered. They should never have taken her in!"

"Lillian Wilson! The Carvers did what they thought was best," Henry responded. "Now, please. Let's not get distracted—"

"It disgusts me!" Lillian talked over her husband, who

rolled his eyes and slouched back on the sofa. "When that filthy Negro couple was hanged, the Carvers should have sent that girl away to—an—an orphanage, where she'd be around her kind. I mean, just think of it! They actually have the nerve to call that Negro their daughter as if she was one of their own children! Just think of the shame their real children must feel having to share the same house with Negro filth, who will only bring humiliation to their family. If you ask me, the Carvers should have let that girl die with her parents."

"Lillian, please!" Henry interrupted in a hushed but severe tone that stressed caution. "The servants." He had always treated his Negroes with respect, and though he did not consider them to be of equal rank as himself, he did not view them as worthless, disgusting animals, either. That was not how he had been raised, and now, as the master of the plantation, he treated his servants with kindness. Lillian also, knowing it meant a great deal to her husband, was usually polite to the servants, although she still could not rid herself of the ardent disdain for their kind that had been drilled in her since she was a little girl.

Feeling she had said all she needed to say on the issue and not wanting to upset Henry any further, Lillian silently took her seat.

When tea was brought in, they both refused it and sat in silence. The fire crackling in the hearth was the only noise that could be heard in the parlor. If the couple had not been so immersed in their thoughts, they would have surely heard the creaking coming from outside the parlor. Two pairs of ears had done their share of listening to the hot discussion, and now two pairs of feet were ascending the groaning stairs back to their beds where they should have been all along.

CHAPTER SEVEN

THE PAST REVEALED

The following day, the Carver and Koch children returned to school, but with a stern warning from their mothers to do everything in their power to avoid the Wilson boys. Robert and James were also given strict orders to not cause any trouble. If they did, they would be severely punished. Thankfully, no problems ensued, though the boys did throw a few scowls Aaron's way.

Back at the Carver cabin, Eliza was enjoying the beautiful spring weather, and every day she found some excuse to spend a good deal of time outdoors. Whether it was completing schoolwork, doing chores, or reading a book, she loved the serenity she found outside of the cabin walls.

She was more than eager, then, when Grace suggested they take a ride into town together. Grace had some things to buy at the mercantile, and she planned on picking up Ellie and Daniel from school on their way home.

"Good afternoon, Mary," Grace greeted her friend. Mrs. Lawson, the previous mercantile owner, had passed away a few years before and her faithful assistant, Mary, now ran the mercantile.

"Oh, hello Grace!" Mary beamed. "Hi Eliza!"

"Hi Mary!" Eliza joyfully responded.

Mary, having been a friend of Grace's since childhood, always treated Eliza and her other children with the utmost kindness as if they were her own. On several occasions, the children would leave the mercantile with a sweet treat, a free gift from Mary. It was this, then, along with Mary's welcoming smile that made Eliza's trips into town so enjoyable. On more than one occasion, too many to count in fact, Eliza had received disapproving scowls and snide remarks from certain townsfolk. Grace and David had spoken with Eliza many times regarding these issues, and Eliza had gotten used to the fact that everywhere she went in life, there were always going to be people who looked down on her because of her color. David and Grace continually reassured Eliza that regardless of skin color, she was just as much a part of their family as Ellie and Daniel were and that they would always love and care for her as their own. It was this promise that helped Eliza to ignore the degrading comments some of the townspeople made and to appreciate the kindness that certain people, like Mary, showed her even more.

Once Mary had gathered all of Grace's items, she leaned across the counter and asked with a knowing smile, "You aren't too old for a licorice stick, are you, Eliza?"

"Hmmm, let me think…" Eliza kidded, putting her hand up to her chin and pretending to seriously contemplate the matter. "Nope. I'm definitely not too old for a licorice stick."

"I didn't think so!" Mary laughed. "Here you go."

"Thanks Miss Mary!"

Eliza took the black licorice and bit off a little chunk.

Just then, Grace saw Mrs. Ludy, who had just settled in the area with her husband. They were a young couple, and Grace had made their acquaintance at church the previous Sunday. While Grace greeted the cheery woman and made small talk, Eliza went out to sit in the wagon, contentedly chewing on her licorice stick.

Once she had finished, two of her fingertips were stained black from the candy. Trying to lick the color off, Eliza soon learned that it wasn't working, so she sat there with her black fingers and now-extra-dark tongue, waiting for her mother.

"Eliza!" she heard someone call her name. Turning, she spotted Aaron waving his hand and running up to the wagon. "What are you doing?"

"Waiting for Mama. She's talking to Mrs. Ludy."

"Hi, Eliza!" Margaret and Ellie quickly joined their older siblings with Daniel and Samuel not far behind them.

"How was school?" Eliza asked.

"Uneventful, thankfully," Ellie answered her sister, letting out a relieved chuckle.

"Robert and James just sat sulking the whole day. It was great!" Aaron laughed, and the others joined in.

"I got a one hundred on my math test, Eliza!" Daniel proudly proclaimed.

"That's great, Daniel," she congratulated, wrapping her arms around his small frame and kissing his head. "I'm so proud of you, and I know Mama will be, too!"

"I'm gonna go tell her!" Without another word, Daniel bounced happily up the mercantile steps with Samuel following.

"Margaret, did you see the new fabrics Miss Mary ordered?" Ellie asked in excitement.

"No."

"She just got them in. Come on! I've got to show you!"

Aaron and Eliza were left alone to engage in a conversation all their own. They were laughing when suddenly, Aaron's face turned serious.

"What is—" Eliza stopped short once she realized the source of Aaron's concern. "Oh no," she moaned.

"Well, if it isn't Little Miss Blackie," Robert degradingly greeted Eliza. "Haven't seen you in town lately."

"She's no concern of yours," Aaron spoke firmly and stood up straighter. "Now go."

Aaron would have defended any of his siblings if they had been insulted, but he felt an extra urge to defend Eliza. She was an easy target for people's insults and sneers because of her color, and Aaron was always ready to protect her if a negative situation should arise.

"Settle down there, Koch," James chimed in. "Robert was just paying his respects to the ugly maiden."

"I heard you boys actually went a whole day without causing any disturbances in the classroom," Eliza piped up with a sneer. "Congratulations. I didn't think it was possible."

"If that was meant to be an insult," Robert steamed, "I've got plenty more for you, slave girl."

"You watch your mouth or I'll be putting my fist in it," Aaron took a step forward, but Eliza's gentle hand on his arm held him back.

"No, Aaron, don't. Fighting doesn't solve anything," Eliza spoke. "What they say doesn't bother me anymore. I've gotten used to their insults, theirs and everyone else's. Let's just go inside."

Just as Eliza turned her back to the bullies, Robert called out devilishly, "Then I guess the fact that your parents were *murdered* and that you now live with a family who never wanted you in the first place doesn't bother you either, huh?"

Eliza stopped dead in her tracks, her blood running cold.

"What are you talking about?" she gasped, almost inaudibly, slowing turning back around.

"You don't know?" Robert sneered. "Your parents were hanged when you were just a baby. The Carvers took you in out of mere obligation and pity. They never really wanted you."

"That's not true," Eliza stammered, her eyes welling with tears.

"It isn't?" Robert smirked. "Why don't you ask them?"

"I'm warning you, Robert," Aaron fumed, clenching his fist.

"My parents love me—"

"Hah!" he mocked. "They're *not* your parents…and they *don't* love you. How could they? Do you think they like having to care for a Negro? You only give your family a bad name."

"Stop it, now!" Aaron shouted.

"Why should I? Everyone knows it's true!" Robert barked. "No white person could ever love a Negro! She's not like us! She doesn't belong here." Turning his hard gaze on Eliza, he hissed, "And she never will."

Eliza felt sick to her stomach. Her heart pounding. Robert's words were more than just insults. They were malicious assaults on everything Eliza had believed, everything her parents had told her over the past fifteen years. She couldn't stay there. With tears streaming down her face, she ran away from the cruel boys as fast as she could.

Aaron was fuming mad as everything in him wanted to attack Robert for this unforgivable treatment of his closest and dearest friend. He glared at Robert, who just smirked back. This last gesture was just too much for Aaron, and he grabbed Robert by the shirt collar and shoved him up against the porch post of the mercantile.

"You scum!" he spat in his face. "If you had any sense at all, you'd—" Aaron stopped, showing more restraint than he had ever shown in his life. He slowly released Robert's shirt and backed away.

"Someday," he foretold, "your actions will come back at you. You reap what you sow."

With that, Aaron ran after Eliza, certain of where she was headed.

*　　*　　*

Just as Eliza and Aaron ran out of town, two strangers appeared on their horses. Their clothes were not tattered and torn, but well-kept. Their boots were polished. Their hair was combed. They weren't slouched over as if defeated or depressed; they sat aright, forcing people to look up at them as they rode by. They received several glances and a few chuckles from some flirtatious women. In response, they tipped their hats and winked, causing even more of a stir. Lots of things had changed since they had left more than twenty years ago. Absorbing all the sights and sounds, they breathed in the fresh air of freedom and smiled.

"Things are gonna be better for us this time, Jake. I can feel it."

"That they are, Max. That they are."

*　　*　　*

"I knew I'd find you here."

Aaron gently approached Eliza, who sat cradling her knees in her arms and sobbing. This spot in the woods, beside the rippling creek and towering pine trees, was where Eliza found solace.

Aaron tried to find the right words to say, but nothing seemed adequate to calm his friend's deep sorrow.

"Don't pay any attention to what they said. None of it's true."

When Eliza didn't respond, Aaron took a seat beside her and put a comforting hand on her back. The water flowing along the bank could barely be heard above Eliza's mournful sobs.

"You know your parents love you, Eliza," Aaron softly reassured her. "They always have and they always will."

"No, Aaron," Eliza whimpered. "They lied to me. They told me my parents died from the fever." She rested her head on her knees and lowered her voice to a small whisper. "They lied to me." Feeling like she had been betrayed, Eliza cried, "How do I know they haven't lied to me about everything else?" A sudden feeling of loneliness overcame her, and for the first time, Aaron noticed a veil seemed to dim her once shining eyes. In a moment, all the light, all her joy was gone. "Robert's right," she bitterly spoke, "I don't belong here. No white person could ever love a Negro, and that's all I'll ever be."

"Eliza—"

"Just go, Aaron," she wept. "Please, just go."

Aaron hesitantly rose from his place. If he had had his way, he would have never left Eliza's side. However, out of respect for her, he willingly yet despondently gave her what she wanted.

Eliza had never felt so alone.

CHAPTER EIGHT

HOME AT LAST

"Excuse me, girl? Could you please tell me who the master of this plantation is?" Jake asked the small, Negro girl from atop his horse. He and Max had just come upon their childhood home, which they hadn't seen in over twenty years.

"Oh," the girl responded in her high, pre-adolescent voice, "that'd be Massa Henry Wilson. A good man, sir. Very good man."

"Thank you, youngin'. Here's something to add to that little pocket of yours," Jake smirked, tossing down a shiny nickel.

"Thank you, sir! Oh, thank you so much!" the girl scurried away to show off her new treasure.

After stopping their horses in front of the house, the brothers dismounted.

"The old place looks just as good as when we left it," Max commented, noticing for the first time in his life just how regal the house was. It amazed him that he could have ever called this place his home. With its large, white columns and wrapped porch, the house had a sophisticated yet welcoming feel. Two rockers, which Max remembered being favorites of his parents, swayed in the wind. How often his mother would sit and relax on warm summer days, working on her needlework or embroidery while the three brothers played contentedly in the yard. He reminisced how the family used to gather on the patio late at night. Henry would play his fiddle while he and Jake would dance merrily and their parents would rock and clap their hands to the rhythm. On occasion, there would be no music, and they would all just peacefully converse and pick out the various constellations in the night sky.

It seems like a lifetime ago, Max thought.

As the brothers ascended the steps leading to the front door, they each took a deep breath, Max out of nervousness, Jake out of proud satisfaction. Then, he knocked.

The knock was heard in the parlor, and Henry rose from his chair, announcing to the maid that he would answer it. When he opened the door, he was clueless to who his visitors were.

"May I help you gentlemen?"

"Henry," Jake quietly responded, almost emotionally, "it's us."

A few seconds lapsed until Henry realized who stood before him. He stepped back in shock.

"Jake?" he barely uttered. "Is it you?"

"It's me…and—"

"Max," Henry finished for him. Tears came to Henry's eyes as he stood face to face with his only family in the world. Once they had run away, Henry had thought he would never see Jake and Max again. And now here they were at his home… at their home.

A flood of emotions overcame him as he embraced his brothers.

"It's so good to see you!" he laughed with joy as tears ran down his face.

"And you, brother," Max said, giving Henry a firm squeeze and pat on the back.

"I just—I just can't believe that you're here after all these years." Henry shook his head in disbelief, smiling bigger than he had in a long time. "Well, come in! Come in!"

Henry led his brothers into the house, and Jake and Max were instantly filled with childhood memories of playing checkers in the parlor, sliding down the banister, and having pie-eating contests.

"Lillian! Lillian, come here! We have company!" Henry beckoned his wife.

"Who?" she asked, scurrying to the front door.

She was greeted with a "Ma'am" from the two gentlemen, who both removed their hats.

When Lillian didn't respond, Henry knew it was because she didn't know what to say. She had no idea who these visitors were, and her countenance showed it.

"Lillian," Henry introduced, "these are my brothers, Jake and Max."

Henry had only discussed his brothers briefly with Lillian, and she hardly knew anything about them, except that they ran away from home when they were seventeen and sixteen. She had never anticipated actually ever meeting them, and now that they were standing in her home, she was quite alarmed.

"Your brothers? Why—it's—" she struggled to find the words to say as she approached them with her hand outstretched. "It's so good to finally meet you."

"I knew Henry would settle down with a nice woman, but I never knew she'd be this pretty," Jake complimented, taking Lillian's hand and kissing it gently.

"Thank you, Mr. Wilson. You're very kind," Lillian acknowledged, quickly withdrawing her hand.

"It's Jake. We are family after all," Jake told her.

"Of course. Thank you, Jake," she smiled.

"It's a pleasure to meet you, Lillian," Max added, taking her hand in his.

"And you as well, Max."

Henry then led them all into the parlor. Jake and Max took seats across from Henry and Lillian.

"I still can't believe that you're here! It feels like a lifetime since I've seen you two!" Henry exclaimed.

"It *has* been," Max reflected.

"Well, tell me everything!" Henry urged. "What have you been up to these past twenty years? What made you come back?"

"To answer your first question," Jake began, "we've traveled all over the country. Most of our time was spent out west, going from town to town. You know me, Henry. I was never content in one place. I had to get out into the world, and I did. There was always something different to see, new people to meet."

"Sounds like quite the adventure," Henry said.

"It was." Jake responded and then paused for effect. "But then, something strange happened. After years of traveling and sight-seeing, I wanted a change of pace. I wanted to settle down and raise a family. I started thinking of my family back home and how much I had missed. So Max and I talked it over, and we decided to come back. We were wrong for leaving, Henry. We were hoping that you could, uh—"Jake paused for a moment. To Henry it appeared that his brother was deeply regretting everything he had done and was trying to find the right words to express himself. Jake, however, was not sorry at all for anything. That's why he paused. Everything in him fought against the words he knew he had to say, but didn't mean at all. He somehow managed to continue with his best acting, "that you could forgive us and that we could start over and be the family that Mother and Father would have wanted us to be."

Jake was eloquent for an outlaw, and his words moved Henry, who was too full of love for his brothers to harbor any bitterness or hate towards them.

"Of course I forgive you!" Tears flowed once again from Henry's eyes as he embraced his brothers. "I'm so glad you're home!"

"So are we," Jake replied, but Henry could not see the smirk on his face.

After a moment, Henry released his brothers, and Jake spoke, "Well, I guess we'd better go into town and find a room for the night."

"Nonsense! You'll stay here with us!" Henry protested.

"No. No, we couldn't impose," Jake refuted.

"It's no imposition at all," Lillian spoke for her husband. "You're family."

"Mother and Father would want it this way," Henry added.

Jake sighed, though in truth, this was exactly what he had hoped would happen.

"Well," he responded, making it seem as though it pained him to impose, "if you insist."

Just then, Robert and James entered, quite surprised to see two strangers in their parlor. Henry was quick to notice his sons and called them over.

"Boys, I want you to meet your Uncle Jake and Uncle Max. They're going to be staying with us for a while."

"Hi," the boys greeted.

"Well, hello boys," Jake responded, shaking both boys' hands. Max did the same.

I bet Jake wasn't expecting this, Max thought. *And two boys at that!*

CHAPTER NINE

HEARTBROKEN

The birds chirped happily in the trees. The creek danced merrily as it rippled against some small stones. The sun peeked through the clouds, shining its brilliant light on everything in its path, except for one lonely creature, who was shaded from its warmth and beauty.

Eliza had been weeping for nearly an hour under the pines, undisturbed. She would have continued to wallow in her despair and loneliness had it not been for a sudden interruption. A twig snapped, and Eliza looked up to behold an unwanted visitor.

"How did you know I was here?" Eliza asked her mother, who was standing just a few feet away.

"Aaron told me," Grace replied tenderly. "He's quite worried about you."

Eliza let out a huff of disgust and turned even further away from her mother. Grace had never seen her daughter like this before, and she took a seat beside her on the soft ground.

"Eliza, what's wrong?"

Grace tried to put her hand on Eliza's shoulder, but she quickly pulled away.

"Eliza, please," Grace pleaded.

"Just leave me alone!" Eliza exclaimed, bursting into tears once again.

It pained Grace tremendously to see her daughter hurting so much.

"Eliza, this doesn't help our relationship when you push me away. If you could just tell me what's wrong, maybe we could—"

"It won't matter! Nothing can change."

"It can if we—"

"No, it can't!" Eliza yelled, clenching her fists and hitting the ground. "You lied to me!"

Grace was clueless as to what Eliza meant, and her harsh response caught her off guard.

"What do you mean? I've never lied to you." Grace protested.

"Why didn't you tell me my parents were murdered?" Eliza cried. "Why would you keep that from me? Why?"

Grace couldn't believe Eliza's words. She and David had done everything in their power to conceal that information from Eliza.

"Who told you that?" Grace questioned, her heart beating rapidly.

"It doesn't matter! All that matters is that it's true, and you lied to me! Why?"

Eliza buried her face in her hands and continued to weep. Her heart was broken, and so was Grace's. Grace had known how much it would hurt Eliza if she knew what had happened to her parents, and that's why she and David had worked so hard to keep it a secret. But Eliza knew now, and there was nothing they could do about it.

"Eliza," Grace whispered, fighting back the tears that she felt coming, "your father and I never meant to hurt you. In fact, that's why we didn't tell you. We knew that you would be deeply hurt. We've always tried to love and protect you the best we knew how. You have to believe that."

"Why should I?" she asked with contempt. "You lied to me about this, so how do I know you aren't lying to me now?"

Grace reached out to touch Eliza's tear-stained cheeks, but she quickly pulled away.

"No!" Eliza shouted. "Don't touch me!"

Grace couldn't restrain her tears any longer. Her daughter was hurting so much, and she felt helpless. Eliza had built a wall between them, and nothing Grace did could change that. How much she wanted to reach out and embrace her daughter—her daughter whom she had loved, nurtured, and cared for as her own. If only Eliza knew how much Grace loved her—how much she had always tried to protect her.

"Eliza," Grace tried to plead once more. "Please. I love you so much…so does your father and—"

"Stop!" Eliza protested angrily. "Don't say anymore! If you truly loved me, you wouldn't have kept this from me all these years."

Eliza looked with disdain at this woman whom she had called "mother" for the past fifteen years. Her heart had grown cold. She was feeling something she had never felt before: hate. Hate for the injustice done to her parents, hate for the lies, and hate for the woman sitting before her now. Curling her lip in bitter disgust, she snapped, "After all, I have a right to know what happened to my *real* parents."

With that last jabbing comment, Eliza ran away, leaving Grace heartbroken and alone.

"Dear God!" Grace pleaded through her tears, collapsing against the trunk of a large pine. "Please help me."

CHAPTER TEN

A HARDENED HEART

"I don't know what we were thinking, Jake," Max muttered, folding his arms behind his neck and resting his head.

Everyone in the house was fast asleep, except for Jake and Max. Max was reclining on the large, feather bed in their bedroom while Jake stood in front of the mirror, getting ready for bed.

"Robert and James change everything."

"Would you quit worrying?" Jake bade his brother to stop talking. "I've got everything under control. Robert and James are far too young to be masters of a plantation."

"They won't always be," Max sighed.

"No. But when Henry has his little accident, we'll be the only candidates for the position. By the time Robert and James *do* come of age, it won't matter because the plantation will be in our hands."

Max huffed in disbelief.

"You make everything sound so simple, Jake."

"This *is* simple, Max. If you had any sense about you at all, you'd think so, too," Jake insulted, running his hands through his hair while admiring himself in the mirror.

"Tomorrow morning we go into town," he announced, flinging his shirt over the chair.

"What for?"

"We're gonna get us some jobs. If we want this whole thing to work out, we gotta make Henry think that we're serious about setting things straight. Taking jobs in town will be just the thing. It'll show Henry that we're dedicated, hard-working—"

"Liars," Max butt in.

Jake scowled at his brother, who in return shifted his gaze down to his twiddling thumbs.

"Don't get smart with me, Max," Jake threatened. "Once we take jobs in town, it'll be the perfect opportunity to earn our reputation back with Henry and get friendly with some of the townspeople. Then, when Henry has his accident, no one will suspect us of anything."

"Alright, I got it. Now if you don't mind, I'd like to get some sleep so I'm not totally dead tomorrow."

Ignoring Jake's irritated mutterings, Max blew out the lamp. His head sunk into the soft pillow, and within minutes, he was sound asleep.

Jake, however, walked over to the window and looked out into the night sky. He could scarcely make out the outlines of the servants' cabins, but he knew they were there. His eyes scanned back and forth across the plantation that was now engrossed in darkness. Enviously evil thoughts filled his mind as he smiled wickedly.

One month, and it'll all be mine!

*   *   *

It was almost ten o'clock. David sat at the kitchen table, tapping his fingers anxiously. Grace paced back and forth, sighing deeply. Ellie and Daniel lay asleep, dreaming peacefully.

There was one family member missing.

Grace had not seen Eliza since she had run away from

her earlier that afternoon. After explaining to David what had happened, Grace told him that it would be best to leave Eliza alone for a little while since she had been so hostile during their conversation. That was before supper time. Now supper was over, the kitchen was cleaned, the children were in bed, and Eliza still had not returned.

"Oh, where could she be?" Grace worried to herself. "David, I'm starting to wonder—"

Grace's words were cut short when the cabin door suddenly creaked open, and a figure stepped into the light.

"Eliza!" Grace exclaimed, though she did not rush to embrace her daughter. As much as she longed to, Eliza had made it clear that afternoon that she desired no affection from Grace.

"Where have you been? It's so late." Grace asked, overcome with mixed emotions.

"I was just…wandering," Eliza said with no emotion. Not wanting to give her mother the satisfaction of an apology or a hint of remorse for what she had done, she added nonchalantly, "but then I got cold, so I came home."

This hurt Grace, for she was hoping that her daughter had come home to make things right. Not knowing how to respond, she stayed silent. David, however, was quite angry.

"Listen here, young lady," he said firmly while controlling his temper. "Just because you're upset does not give you the right to run off like that, and the way you treated your mother is not allowed. As your parents, we deserve your respect. Now, go to bed, and we'll discuss your punishment in the morning."

"I don't know why I even bothered coming home!" Eliza declared, marching into her room and slamming the door behind her.

"David," Grace whispered, taking her husband's arm, "what are we going to do?"

"I don't know," he sighed, softly patting Grace's hands. "I just don't know."

Inside the bedroom, Eliza plopped down on her bed, mumbling spiteful comments.

"Eliza, is that you?" Ellie asked sleepily.

Throwing her shoes on the floor, Eliza angrily responded, "Yah, Ellie. Now, just go back to bed."

"I was worried about you. We all were. If you want to talk about anything," Ellie offered, "I'm always here."

"I don't want to talk, alright?" Eliza snapped. "I don't want to talk to anyone ever again. Now just leave me alone!"

Ellie sat still, stunned by her sister's behavior. She and Eliza had always been so close. Why was she pushing her away? The darkness of night hid Ellie's face from view, for which she was thankful. Never before had Eliza made her cry.

The next morning, Eliza awoke and felt no different. Bitterness and discontentment had overcome her, and she was oblivious to just how much.

When breakfast was served, she remained in her room until she was sternly told to join the rest of the family with the promise that she would be punished if she didn't.

She scowled through the meal. She did not thank Grace for her food. She did not bow her head for prayer. When the meal was finished, she did not offer to help clear the table.

No one knew what to say or rather, how to say what they wanted. Therefore, they remained silent. That is, until David finally spoke.

"Eliza, would you please come outside with me?" His voice

was authoritative yet gentle.

"No, thank you," she responded, turning her head away.

"It's not an option."

David opened the door and stood beside it, waiting for his daughter to come. When Eliza saw he wasn't budging, she rose from her chair and followed him outside.

It was a beautiful spring morning. The sun shone brightly. The wind whistled through the swaying trees. The birds sung merrily, dancing through the air. Everything in creation seemed to sing with joy, except for Eliza.

Both David and Eliza were silent for a few moments. Leaning up against a fence post, David pondered what to say to his troubled daughter. He knew she was upset, and he didn't want to say or do anything to provoke her further. However, he was wise enough to know that ignoring the problem would not lead to a resolution. He had to say something. He just hoped it would be right.

"Eliza," he softly began, "you realize that as a family, we discuss our problems together. We don't shut each other out. That doesn't help anyone, and it certainly doesn't help the problems go away. Do you understand?"

Eliza nodded, though she did not look at her father.

"You also need to understand that as your parents we desire the very best for you. It pains your mother and me very much to see you hurting like this." David paused, and for the first time since he had begun talking, Eliza looked at him. His eyes were filled with concern for her, and her heart softened—though, just a little.

"Would you please tell me what's bothering you?"

Eliza's eyes started to fill with tears again, and she quickly turned away so her father wouldn't see.

"Lots of things," she responded, doing her best to restrain herself from crying. "It's just—you both lied to me. For fifteen years, you've lied to me. And now it—it hurts. It really, really hurts." A sickening pain shot through Eliza's stomach, and she couldn't contain herself any longer. The floodgate of tears burst open, and Eliza buried her head in her hands. David's heart ached for his daughter, and he wrapped his arms around her.

"Your mother and I did what we thought was best. We wanted to protect you," he tried to comfort, but she pushed away.

"Protect me from what? The truth? How could you possibly think you were helping me by lying to me about my parents?" she cried.

"Because we knew if we told you the truth, it would upset you…like it is right now."

A moment of silence lapsed between them. Both felt so differently about the situation, yet both were hurting. While Eliza's hurt was out of bitterness, David's was out of love.

"Eliza," he gently continued, "as parents, we sometimes have to make hard decisions. This was one of them. We didn't see the benefit in telling you about your parents. What we did see was the hurt that it would cause, and we wanted to spare you from that."

Eliza wiped the tears from her face and held her head higher to show her father that she was not succumbing to his supposedly loving gestures. Refusing to swallow her pride, she retained her solemn gaze into the endless countryside in front of her.

David sensed her coldness. For the first time in his life,

he felt completely helpless. What could he say? What could he do to change her mind? Nothing. That was the stinging answer. Against a hardened heart, he could do nothing.

As he turned to walk back toward the cabin, he felt compelled to say one last thing.

"Your mother and I have only ever loved you, Eliza. You're our daughter, and nothing will ever change that."

CHAPTER ELEVEN

FOR BETTER AND FOR WORSE

After awaking from a long night of peaceful sleep, the Wilson family gathered around the table for breakfast. Henry could barely contain his joy at having his brothers back with him, and his beaming smiled conveyed it. Lillian couldn't recall ever seeing her husband so enthused.

"Morning everyone!" Jake exclaimed as he and Max entered the dining room. All the places were already set, and a delicious aroma filled the room.

"Morning!" Henry responded, shining with excitement.

"I hope you both were comfortable," Lillian told her guests.

"Most comfortable," Jake responded in his flattering tone. "I do believe that was the best night of sleep I've ever had."

"I'd have to agree," Max added.

"Well, I'm glad to hear it. Please sit down," Lillian offered.

"Thank you."

Taking their seats at the table, Jake and Max were eager to eat the scrumptious food in front of them. It had been years since they had had a home-cooked meal.

"I'd forgotten how delicious home-made bread smells," Jake said as Lillian passed him the butter dish.

"Everything looks so good," Max complimented, filling his plate.

"Eat as much as you'd like," Lillian said. She didn't have to tell them twice.

Both men were so hungry that it took all the manners they

could muster to restrain themselves from being total slobs so as not to offend their hosts. The food was delicious, and the brothers could not get enough of it.

While Jake and Max were busy eating, Robert and James took the opportunity to bring up a topic that was on both of their minds.

"Father! Guess what?" Robert declared. "Jade Williams just got a rifle!"

"It's a beauty," James exclaimed, "and he's only thirteen!"

"Is that so?" Henry asked, taking a bite of his eggs.

"Yah," Robert paused, looking at his brother, who motioned for him to continue. "Father, James and I were thinking that maybe we could get our own rifles."

"Maybe our own revolvers, too!" James added, pushing their luck even further.

"And how do you expect to pay for those?" Henry asked matter-of-factly.

"Well, we were kind of hoping you'd pay for 'em."

Henry nearly choked on his food, and his eyes widened.

"And why would I do that?"

Robert and James exchanged confused glances believing they were entitled to receiving a new expensive rifle.

"Just because," Robert answered.

Henry's eyes bulged even more.

"That's a pretty expensive 'just because' gift, don't you think?" Henry asked with an annoyed chuckle, taking a sip of water.

"Okay," Robert consented. "An early birthday gift?"

"Your birthday's not for two more months."

Robert and James weren't giving up so easily. Once they

had their minds made up, it was hard to dissuade them.

"Yah, but it's not like we're asking you to buy just anything. I mean, shooting is a valuable life skill. Every man should have his own gun."

"I agree with you," Henry said, but the boys knew he wasn't giving in to their argument. "When you two become *men* and stop behaving like boys, you may have your own guns. Until then, you have no need for weapons."

Jake had been listening intently to the conversation since shooting was something he had had a great deal of practice in.

"Now, wait a second, Henry," he joined in. "I do agree with you that a new rifle is an expensive gift and that it should be given only on special occasions. But I have to agree with the boys in that shooting is a necessary life skill. You never know what kind of scrape you might find yourself in, what kind of people you might encounter. It's a safety matter. Therefore," he announced, firmly planting his hands on the table and raising his voice, "if you boys are interested, I'd be willing to train you both on how to properly handle and operate a gun." He then shifted his gaze back to his brother. "With your permission that is, Henry."

"Oh, please, Father?" Robert pleaded.

"Yes, please?!?" James added.

Henry searched his wife's expression, silently asking for her consent. She smiled softly and nodded. While he was not fully convinced that allowing the boys to handle a weapon was a good idea, Henry had Lillian's approval, and that's all he needed.

"Alright, even though it's against my better judgement. But school work and chores must come first, and if you misbehave or cause any trouble, you won't get to do it anymore. Do you understand?"

The boys nodded excitedly, and Jake looked content.

"When can we start, Uncle Jake?" James asked enthused.

"How about this afternoon?"

"Yes!" Robert cheered.

"Off you boys go to school now," Henry said, and before he had a chance to say anything else, the boys jumped out of their seats, grabbed their books, and ran out the door.

"I've never seen them so excited," Lillian chuckled. "Thank you for doing this, Jake. I know it means a lot to them."

"Don't mention it," Jake smiled, and Max eyed his brother without turning his head. He knew this was all part of Jake's plan to gain the family's approval and trust. But it seemed wrong. Very wrong.

"Well, Max and I better be on our way," Jake announced, rising from his chair.

"Where are you going?" Henry asked.

"Into town. We thought since we're gonna be here for a while, it would be a good idea to get us some jobs."

"Let me come with you," Henry offered, standing up. "I know most of the townsfolk. I could probably work something out for you both."

"You don't have to do that, Henry; you've done enough already," Jake countered. "Besides, this is something Max and I need to do on our own."

"If that's the way you feel."

"It is," Jake assured his brother. "Thank you for breakfast. It was the best we've had in a long time."

"Yes, thank you," Max said.

"I'm glad you both enjoyed it," Lillian replied with a charming smile.

With that, Jake and Max left. A Negro boy led them to the stables where their horses had been brushed and fed. Jake gave the boy a coin and thanked him for his help.

Wow, Max thought. *He's trying really hard to be nice. Too hard.*

The ride into town was peaceful. Both brothers were silent for most of the way. When they arrived at the lumber mill, they both dismounted and tied their horses to a fence post. After asking to speak with the man in charge, they were led into a small office where a short, stout man sat writing at a desk. His face was round and plump and most of his hair was gone. He had a good smile, though, and the brothers thought they might be in luck.

"What can I do for you gentlemen?" asked Mr. Lewis. Small dimples formed on each side of his mouth as he grinned widely.

"Well, sir," Jake started, "my name is Jake, Jake Wilson, and this is my brother Max."

"Say," Mr. Lewis said, leaning forward and pointing a fat finger at the brothers, "you two wouldn't happen to be related to Henry Wilson, would ya'?"

"As a matter of fact, we are. He's our younger brother. We came to town to see him, and we plan on staying for a while."

"I see," Mr. Lewis leaned back in his chair and shook his finger. "I thought I saw a family resemblance, and then when you told me your name that confirmed it for me." Tilting his head and eyeing Jake and Max, he asked, "So what can I help you with, boys?"

"We're actually looking for a job, Mr. Lewis, and we were

wondering if you could use any extra help."

"You don't say?" Mr. Lewis asked. He paused and rose from his chair. The brothers waited for him to speak. Taking a few steps forward, he tapped his pointer finger on his mouth as if he were thinking. "Funny thing you boys should come in today," he said, motioning to the brothers. "Some might call it luck; I call it Providence. You see, one of my men just got seriously injured and has been confined to his bed for at least a couple of weeks. We've got a big order to fulfill, and I could really use the help. I was just getting ready to put this sign out front," he said, holding up a "Help Wanted" board. "Looks like I won't be needing it, though," Mr. Lewis smiled and extended his hand to Jake. "You're hired."

"Thank you, sir!" Jake beamed, shaking his hand. Max did the same.

"No, thank *you*, boys! I could use four extra hands on the job. Now, follow me, and let's get you two to work."

"Yes, sir!" the brothers simultaneously responded.

*   *   *

Back at the Carver's cabin, a lonely silence filled the atmosphere. Grace was slowly rolling out dough for an apple pie, but her mind was wandering through troubled places.

Behind the door on the other side of the room was her daughter, writhing with bitterness and grief. Between mother and daughter had formed a wall, a wall that seemed impossible to tear down. Earlier that morning, Grace had attempted to console and caress Eliza, who responded coldly to her mother's love. She wanted nothing to do with anyone. She just wanted to be alone, to scorn the world and her very existence. She wished to be anywhere but home, anywhere that would take her away from the familiar faces that reminded her she would never be like them.

Her attitude cut deep into Grace's soul. Next to the Lord and her husband, she loved nothing more than her children. To see one of them hurting this deeply pained her more than she could bear. Her heart cried, and a single tear dropped from her face onto the dough below.

There was a soft knock at the cabin door. Grace wiped her floury hands on her apron and dabbed the moisture from her eyes. Opening the door, she beheld her mother, smiling ear to ear.

"Hi, Mama," Grace forced a smile.

"Hello, dear," Mrs. Johnson embraced her daughter and kissed her gently on the cheek.

After inviting her inside, Grace asked, "What are you doing here?"

Mrs. Johnson held up a bundle with brown wrapping and tied with string.

"It's that time again," she announced.

Grace chuckled and received the package from her mother. She shook it, pretending not to know what it was.

"Hmmm," she queried. "Is it a new dress?"

Mrs. Johnson played along, shaking her head.

"A book? A new frying pan maybe?"

"Oh, just open it, you silly girl!"

Grace carefully unwrapped the package as her mother watched in anticipation. As she tore the last piece of paper off, Grace pulled out a lovely, light blue afghan.

"Mama, it's beautiful," Grace told her. "I think it's some of your best work yet."

"Well, I *have* had plenty of practice, you know."

"One for each grandchild," Grace grinned, petting the soft material.

"I love them all so very much."

Mrs. Johnson spoke those words out of the utmost tenderness and affection. Her tone touched Grace, forcing her to remember the child who wouldn't accept her love. She didn't want her mother to see she was upset, yet she couldn't dismiss the ache in her heart. Hugging the afghan against her chest, she began to cry.

Mrs. Johnson didn't know what to make of her daughter's sudden change in mood. Helping Grace sit down, she asked what was wrong.

"It's Eliza," Grace whispered through her tears, not wanting her daughter to hear their conversation.

"What about Eliza? Is she sick?" Mrs. Johnson's face instantly became worried.

"No, it's worse than that." Grace paused, choking back her emotion so she could continue. "She's upset because she's been lied to."

"By whom?"

"David and me, for not telling her the truth about her parents' deaths. She's so angry and insists that she had a right to know and that it was wrong for us to keep it from her."

"But you were only doing it to protect her. She has to know that."

"We tried to tell her, but she wouldn't listen." Grace

attempted to speak, but she was choked up.

Lifting her hand gently to her daughter's face, Mrs. Johnson brushed the tears away.

"I'm here for you, Grace," she tried to comfort, stroking Grace's cheek.

"I know, Mama," she whimpered. "It's just, I feel so helpless. This has to be the worst feeling in the world: seeing your child in such despair, watching them pull away from you, and not being able to do anything. I can't seem to get her back, Mama," she cried, silently pleading for her mother's help. "She won't talk to anyone. She barely leaves her room. She won't let me hug her or kiss her," Grace said those words with even more anguish than the rest. "It's not natural. A mother is supposed to love on her child. And she won't let me! She just seems so angry, so discontent. I don't know what to do."

Mrs. Johnson gazed into her daughter's worried eyes, full of sadness and loneliness. To see Grace hurting this much caused a deep pain in her own soul. Such is a mother's love.

"What if Eliza spent the day with me tomorrow?" Mrs. Johnson suggested. "I think it would do her some good to get out of the cabin. We could do some baking together; she always enjoyed that. It might help take her mind off of things."

"You think it will help?" Grace asked, a spark of hope shimmering in her eyes.

"It's worth a try."

Grace leaned into her mother's arms, sighing with relief. "Thank you, Mama."

"I love you, Grace," Mrs. Johnson stroked her hair as she used to do when Grace was a young girl and placed a tender kiss on her forehead.

"I love you, too, Mama."

CHAPTER TWELVE

A FRESH START

"Alright, boys!" Mr. Lewis called out to his tired workers. "That's it for today. You all put in a good day's work, especially you two," he said, turning towards Jake and Max. "I'd call your first day on the job a success."

"Thank you, sir," Jake responded, shaking Mr. Lewis's hand.

"Now get outta here, all of you," he shouted, shooing them away with his hands. The men all knew it was in good humor, for his smile conveyed it. "Go home to your families, and get some rest. You'll need it. We've got another hard day tomorrow."

Receiving simultaneous replies from his crew, Mr. Lewis went to lock up the office.

Jake and Max sighed, each exhausted from a strenuous day's labor. Swiping his shirt sleeve across his sweaty brow, Jake said, "I'm just about out of chew." With a snort, he spit a chunk out. "Think I'll run over to the mercantile and pick some up."

Just then, Robert and James ran up with glowing smiles on their faces, a very rare sight.

"Hi, Uncle Jake! Hi, Uncle Max!" the boys exclaimed.

"Hi there," Jake responded. "What are you boys doing?"

"School just let out. Can you give us our shooting lessons now, Uncle Jake? Can you?" There was no beating around the bush. The boys were eager to have their uncle train them, and they were determined to get their way.

"I can get your chew for you if you want," Max offered. "You go on ahead with them."

Jake looked from his brother to his nephews and quickly responded, "Alright then."

With hoots and hollers, the boys headed home with their uncle, leaving Max to shop on his own. He didn't mind it, though. It was one of the rare times he was without his brother's presence, something that lately he had been growing to strongly dislike. While Jake was usually good at putting up a front for others, he wasn't afraid to show his true colors around Max. He was cold, angry, greedy, always wanting something more, something different from what he had. He was never content; he never had been, even when he was a child.

What had started as discontentment had grown into something much darker. Such is the way with sin. When left to itself, it never goes away; it always grows. It grows into a consuming darkness, one that cannot be penetrated with anything but the Light. Those ensnared by the bondage of sin are hopelessly lost. Their souls enslaved to it.

Max saw how bitterness and greed had consumed his brother. He saw what he was willing to do to get his way, and Max felt helpless to stop it. He couldn't tell anyone. Saying anything against Jake to his face would mean certain outrage and likely harm to Max. Saying anything against Jake to others could mean jail for both of them, or worse. He had to keep silent. He had to go along with his brother's wicked scheme.

Trying his best to enjoy his short reprieve from Jake's constant presence, Max inhaled deeply and walked up the steps to the mercantile. As he entered, his eyes met those of an attractive woman. They retained each other's gaze for a moment, unsure of why they each felt they knew the other. After it became slightly awkward, they smiled politely and resumed their business. As Max walked through the small store to where he guessed the chewing tobacco would be, he could not get the woman's face out of his mind. Her large kind eyes and gentle smile...they were familiar. He knew her, but how?

After grabbing two packs of chewing tobacco, he turned around to see the same young woman checking out at the counter. He studied her for a moment. Her chestnut hair was pulled back neatly in a low bun with just a few strands hanging loose, complementing her petite face. With large brown eyes and a small nose, she was a sight to see, especially for Max, who had long been denied the pleasure of being in the presence of ladies.

The woman thanked the mercantile owner and placed her purchases in her basket.

"Have a nice day, Katelyn," Mary said with a smile.

"You, too, Mary," Katelyn replied, and she exited the store.

Max stood frozen. It had been over twenty years since he had last seen Katelyn. Here she had been only a few feet away from him, and he hadn't even known it. The joy he was feeling could not be contained, and a smile appeared on his face. Chuckling in disbelief and pure joy, he tossed one of the packs of chewing tobacco up in the air.

Wearing her same charming smile, Mary greeted Max as he approached the counter to check out. Her joy was contagious and widened the already big smile that Max was wearing.

"Will this be all for you sir?" she asked.

Max told her it would be and gave her the money. After closing the drawer to the cash register and handing Max his change, she enquired, "Are you new to town?"

"Yes and no," Max responded, causing Mary to wonder. "I was born and raised here, but then I left for a while. Now I'm back hopefully to stay."

"You have family here, then?"

"Yes, my brother Henry Wilson, his wife, Lillian, and their two kids."

"I thought you looked familiar!" Mary responded enthusiastically. "Are you Jake?"

"Max. Jake's my older brother."

"You were the one who used to sit behind Katelyn Barton in school and pull her pigtails!" Mary announced, recalling the funny scene.

"Yup, that was me."

"Seems like a lifetime ago."

Max didn't say anything in response, and his face became more solemn. The carefree, happy days of his childhood were so many years before. Now, he had a chance to start over. Could things really ever go back to normal? To the way it used to be when he was a boy?

"Speaking of Katelyn, wasn't that her that just left a few minutes ago?" he quickly asked, not wanting Mary to notice the discomfort her statement had caused him.

"Yes. She had to pick up some fabric and glue for a school project."

"She's the teacher then?"

"Mmm-hm," Mary told him. "She has been for the past— oh, I'd say—seven, eight years, maybe. The kids love her."

They're not the only ones, Max thought to himself.

"Well, thank you," Max said, grabbing the tobacco and starting to leave.

"Of course. And welcome home."

Max stopped in his tracks and turned around to look her in the eyes.

"Thank you," he said, a sudden peace sweeping over him. *Home. This is my home.*

*   *   *

At the plantation, Jake was teaching the boys how to properly draw and shoot a gun. It was hard to tell who was having more fun.

"Good, Robert," Jake complimented him on his quick draw. "Now as you push the gun out from you, you're gonna cock the hammer. Perfect! Like that. Then, you want to pivot on the trigger guard."

"Like this?" Robert asked, attempting unsuccessfully to follow his uncle's instructions.

"Not quite. Let me show you," Jake said, taking the gun from Robert. He and James watched carefully, wanting to master everything their uncle taught them.

"You see?" he asked the boys, who nodded. "Now you try."

This time, Robert got it right. Jake gave him a firm slap on the back. After James had his turn and also succeeded, Jake let out a hearty laugh.

"You both are experts at this!" he declared.

"We'll never be as good as you, Uncle Jake," James said dejectedly.

"With lots of practice, and luck, you might get to be even better than me."

Just then, Max rode up on his horse. Dismounting, he handed the chewing tobacco to Jake, who didn't even bother to thank him.

Once inside the confines of his bedroom, he let out a boyish squeal of delight. Seeing Katelyn had made his stomach all knotted up and his heart turned upside down.

"Tomorrow." He determined that the following day he would go see Katelyn at the school.

"I wonder if she'll remember me," he whispered to himself. "What should I say? Hello Miss Barton...nooooo, that's too formal. Hello Katelyn. Well, maybe. Oh, man!"

With his mind racing and his heart pounding, he set to work on just the right thing to say to her. It had to be perfect.

*   *   *

A soft tap resounded throughout the room. The curtains were pulled. The young girl sat in darkness. Without receiving an answer, the inquisitor opened the door.

"Eliza?" Aaron stood in the doorway. Upon hearing his kind voice, Eliza turned her head to see him.

"Aaron?" she quietly asked. Although she wouldn't have admitted it, part of her was happy to see him and that he cared.

"Eliza, we just finished our homework," he spoke gently, sitting down on the bed next to her. "We're gonna play a game of hide-n-seek. I thought maybe you'd like to come out with us?" His tone urged her to participate, and if it weren't for her pride, she would have consented.

"I can't," she replied, turning away.

"Why not?" Aaron was angered at her stubbornness. More than that, he was concerned for her. "Locking yourself in your room isn't going to change anything, and it's not gonna make you feel any better. You're shutting the people out that care about you the most."

Eliza shook her head in protest, refusing to acknowledge the fact she knew to be true.

"Please, just go."

Aaron lingered a moment longer, staring at the one who used to be his closest friend. When he saw that Eliza wasn't budging, he stood to leave. As he reached the door, he stopped.

"What did I ever do to you?" he questioned. "I thought we were friends."

Hearing those words hurt Eliza. As much as she wanted to admit she had been wrong and join Aaron, she could not bring herself to do it.

"I just need some time alone," she whispered, pleading with him to try to understand.

Without answering, Aaron left the room, closing the door behind him. As soon as he appeared in the kitchen, Daniel rushed to his side.

"What did she say?" he asked, a glimmer of hope sparkling in his young eyes.

"She's not coming, Daniel. I'm sorry."

Hanging his head dismally, Daniel aimlessly swung his wooden sword around. Ellie and Margaret both sighed.

"I feel so bad for her," Margaret said.

"It's her own choice, Margaret," Grace told her as she took a fresh loaf of homemade bread out of the oven. "It doesn't have to be this way. Her attitude is in her control and no one else's."

After a short moment of silence, all of the children went outside to play their game, though at first, none of them were really in the mood.

Grace took this opportunity to speak with Eliza, even though she was sure she didn't want anything to do with her.

She hesitantly approached Eliza, offering up a silent prayer as she did so.

"They were all really disappointed when you didn't play with them," Grace said, and, surprisingly, Eliza faced her mother when she spoke. For a moment, Grace thought she saw regret in her daughter's expression. In fact, she was sure that's what it was.

"They'll still have fun," Eliza stated, trying to cover any trace of emotion. However, she failed miserably.

"They'd have more fun if you were with them," Grace rebutted. Taking a deep breath, she continued, "Grandma stopped by today. She asked if you'd like to spend the day with her tomorrow, just you two."

As upset as Eliza was, her heart softened when her grandma was mentioned. Eliza had adored her for as long as she could remember, and she had never suffered a lack of affection while in her grandma's presence. She always felt special when her grandma was around. Her warm hugs, gentle kisses, even the fresh-smelling aroma of her clothes, nothing could compare to them. Even the food at her house tasted better.

Usually all three children were together, so Eliza rarely got alone time with her grandma. The idea that she could have her all to herself for a whole day excited her. Her joy was quickly quenched, however, when she thought of what the reason could be for such a proposal.

"Why would she invite me over *now*?"

"I think she's just missing spending time with you. It will be nice for you two to have some alone time."

"Yah…I guess."

Not sure what else to say, Grace stood to leave.

"Supper will be ready in a little bit," she said, hoping Eliza wanted to join them.

"Okay," was Eliza's response, and Grace left the bedroom feeling somewhat hopeful.

CHAPTER THIRTEEN

THE GARDEN

As the sun began to peak over the horizon, David and Grace grasped each other's hands and prayed for the strength, peace, and wisdom to begin yet another day. This had been their routine every morning since they were first married. It helped to not only strengthen their relationship as a couple, but also as brother and sister in Christ, striving to encourage one another in their walk with Him.

This morning in particular, they focused most of their prayer time on Eliza. Next to the Lord's perfect, selfless love for His children, there is no greater love than that of a mother for her child. David had seen his wife's struggle over the last few days, and he assured her that they would work this out together, that she wouldn't have to walk through it alone. They sought the Lord's help. They pleaded with Him to soften Eliza's heart, to restore her joy, to open her eyes once again to see how much they cared for her but, most importantly, how much *He* cared for her.

They desperately hoped that today would bring a change.

Eliza was quiet at breakfast, though she did not seem as melancholy as she had been the past two days. This was an encouragement to David and Grace.

After the meal was finished, David set to work on the farm. Ellie and Daniel left for school, and Eliza headed to the Johnson's house. Grace was alone. Not wanting to succumb to the loneliness, she did the only thing she knew could bring comfort.

She prayed.

*   *   *

"Eliza, come in!" Mrs. Johnson welcomed her granddaughter. When she extended her arms, Eliza did not refuse her. How could she? Mrs. Johnson had never shown Eliza anything but love.

"I'm really looking forward to today!" Mrs. Johnson exclaimed.

"Me, too," Eliza responded with a grin.

"I thought we could do some baking, maybe play some checkers. What do you say?"

"Sounds good to me."

Though Eliza wasn't leaping for joy, she did seem to be happy, at least somewhat. Mrs. Johnson was determined to make this an enjoyable time, one that would bring Eliza back to her normal self.

The hours flew by as grandmother and granddaughter baked, talked, and even laughed together. Chocolate pie was a family favorite and was, therefore, the choice of the day. Mrs. Johnson also decided to bake a loaf of homemade bread, which Eliza helped her make. By the time they were finished, both of them were spotted with flour, but they didn't care. They were too engaged in their checkers match to notice their disheveled appearances. Eliza had won the first three games, and they were now starting their fourth.

"I don't know how you do it, Eliza!" Mrs. Johnson declared. "I've been playing checkers since I was a little girl and you still manage to beat me every single time."

"I've had lots of practice," she said with a chuckle.

"I remember when I used to play with your mother. We'd

play games for hours in the evenings. Checkers was always her favorite. She was good, too."

Eliza set down the checker piece she had been fiddling with, and a sudden gloominess came over her.

"I don't think I want to play anymore, Grandma."

Mrs. Johnson pushed the checker board to the side and studied her granddaughter for a moment. Based on what Grace had told her the day before, she knew Eliza was troubled. Mrs. Johnson was actually surprised when Eliza showed up and wore a smile throughout the course of the day. It seemed like she was genuinely enjoying herself. What had changed?

"What's wrong, Eliza?"

"It's nothing. Really."

"Well that's not true," Mrs. Johnson refuted. "You don't quit a checkers game over nothing, especially when you're winning."

Eliza sighed. She knew her grandma would not give up until she had an honest answer.

"It's just…a few days ago, I went into town with Mama, and while we were there, Robert and James, the school bullies, they told me some things." Eliza paused, replaying the horrible scene in her mind. Feelings of grief and anger once again overcame her. "Turns out those things were true, even though I didn't believe them at first."

"What did they tell you?" Mrs. Johnson's countenance became downcast, and her eyes flooded with anguish.

"That…" Eliza struggled to say the words that filled her with such grief and anger and despair. "That my parents were murdered and that Mama and Father took me in out of obligation."

"Eliza, dear," Mrs. Johnson pleaded, "your parents love you. They always have, and they always will."

"They shouldn't have lied to me. It would have been better to hear it from them than to hear it from those...those—" Eliza couldn't finish her words, and her grandma reached across the table to grasp her hand.

"It's so hard, Grandma! For the first time in my life," she raised her eyes to meet her grandma's, and with a voice trembling with hopelessness, she whispered, "I don't feel like I belong here."

Trying to maintain her composure and pride, she sat up straighter and said, "You know, people have said things in the past, and I just haven't paid much attention to them. Mama always said not to. That people would always say mean things, and she was right. But never before had I heard anything that hurt me as much as that." Eliza's voice cracked and she swallowed hard to keep herself from crying.

"Your parents wanted to protect you, Eliza. They were only doing what they thought was best, and it's not always easy," Mrs. Johnson said, with a look that conveyed she had had to make many difficult decisions in her lifetime.

"Do you think it's easy for me? I've grown up my whole life in a family who never wanted me, in a place where I don't fit in."

"That's not true, Eliza."

"Yes, it is, Grandma. It'd be better for everyone if I weren't here."

Mrs. Johnson sat back in her chair and thought of what else she could say. It wasn't so much anger for being lied to that Eliza was feeling as much as it was discontentment.

Suddenly, an idea came to mind.

"Come with me," she said, rising from her chair.

"Where?"

"You'll see."

Opening the door, Mrs. Johnson stood, waiting for Eliza to follow her. Hesitantly, Eliza got up and walked outside.

Mrs. Johnson led them both to her garden where cucumbers, tomatoes, cabbage, garden peas, sweet potatoes, onions, carrots, and beets were growing in abundance. Mrs. Johnson loved gardening, and Eliza enjoyed helping her collect the harvest each year.

"I thought we weren't bringing them in for a few more weeks yet," Eliza said, confused when her grandma bent down next to one of the tomato plants.

"We're not," Mrs. Johnson replied. "Tell me, Eliza: how did this tomato plant start out?"

"Um...as a seed?" Eliza was totally perplexed. Her grandma knew that she was familiar with plants. Why was she giving her a gardening lesson?

"That's right." Mrs. Johnson tenderly stroked the leaves of the plant in a way that only a gardener would. "And who planted that seed?"

"You did."

Raising her eyes to meet Eliza's, Mrs. Johnson said, "I planted this seed, this garden, exactly where I wanted it. I could have just as easily planted it over near the barn where the plants would be trampled on and die. But that's not what a good gardener does. He picks the best patch of land he can find where he knows his plants will not only grow but thrive."

Eliza looked at her grandma and then at the tomato plant.

She was starting to understand her illustration.

"When weeds sprout up," Mrs. Johnson continued, motioning at one by her foot, "the gardener pulls them out." With that, she yanked the weed from the ground. "A good gardener doesn't just plant his garden and then leave it to take care of itself. He waters and nurtures it and protects it from harm. But the plant has a job, too. It needs to take what it's been given—sunlight, water, nutrients—and use them to sustain itself. The gardener can't do everything for the plant; it has some responsibility of its own."

Lifting her gaze from the plant to her granddaughter, she said, "The Lord has you exactly where He wants you, Eliza. He's a God of order, a God of perfection. There's no randomness or blind chance with Him, and He never makes mistakes. He knew that right here is where you would grow best. Your job is to grow where you've been planted. You need to take what you've been given and use it for His glory. And when those weeds of discontentment and bitterness start to grow, you need to ask the Lord to replace it with a heart of gratitude and forgiveness. He's given you so much, Eliza: a warm home, good health, a family that has adopted you and loves—"

"That's just it, grandma!" Eliza interrupted. "I'm *adopted*!" Lowering her head, she whispered, "I'll never be their real family."

Mrs. Johnson stood and walked over to Eliza. Placing her hands gently on Eliza's shoulders, she said, "Adoption is a beautiful thing, Eliza. It's when a family chooses a child to be their own, not out of obligation, but out of love." Tilting

Eliza's chin upward to meet her gaze, Mrs. Johnson continued, "It's what the Lord has done for us. 'Behold, what manner of love the Father hath bestowed on us, that we should be called the sons of God.'"

"First John chapter three verse one," mumbled Eliza.

Mrs. Johnson nodded, impressed that Eliza knew the reference.

"The Lord has called us to be His children. He *adopted* us into His family. Nothing in us makes us worthy to be called His children. He wasn't obligated to do it. He did it out of love." Mrs. Johnson held Eliza's focus as she said, "There is no shame in being adopted, Eliza. If anything, it should give you, and give me, great joy and gratitude. The Lord doesn't make mistakes. In the same way that He ordained you to be a part of His family, He has ordained Grace and David Carver to be your parents. You need to rest in that, Eliza, and be content where He's placed you, right here, right now."

Eliza's eyes began to fill with tears as she realized the truthfulness in her grandma's words. However, she still felt a deep hole in her heart, and she didn't know how to fill it.

"Grandma…I," Eliza stuttered, trying to convey her emotions. "I just, I feel like, how can anything ever go back to the way it was now that I know?"

Mrs. Johnson brushed away Eliza's tears, and with all the love and sympathy she had to offer, she answered, "You need to stop focusing on the past…because that's exactly where it is. I know it hurts, but you *can't* change it, Eliza. What you *can* change is what's happening *now*. You can fix your relationship with your parents and your siblings."

"It's just so painful, grandma! That memory is there forever. I don't know how I can ever be happy again."

With this last comment, Mrs. Johnson straightened herself and her tone turned from one of sympathy to one of tender yet stern instruction.

"Look at me, Eliza. Happiness doesn't last. When something goes wrong, when someone we love leaves us, happiness is gone. It's only a feeling we get when things are going our way. Joy is different. It lasts forever, and it can *only* be found in Jesus, being content with His promises, with His Word, with His sovereign plans for our lives. See, joy…it's like a treasure chest, and contentment is the key. Very few people in this life ever have true joy, and that's because very few people learn contentment. They're always looking to change things, wishing their lives were different from the way they are. I don't want that to be you, Eliza, and I know you don't want that either."

"No, I don't."

"Then trust that He knows what's best, and be content with what's He's given you, right here, right now, and He will fill you with the joy only He can give."

When her grandma finished speaking, Eliza felt a tremendous sorrow lifted from her heart. She felt hopeful, and it seemed like all the pain was gone as she collapsed in her grandma's arms. Stroking Eliza's head, Mrs. Johnson reassured her that everything would be alright. In that moment, Eliza could feel nothing but overwhelming love.

"I love you, grandma," she cried.

"I love you, too, Eliza."

NEW BEGINNINGS

As the afternoon came to a close, Max grew more excited and more nervous. The thought of not only seeing Katelyn but also having a conversation with her made his pace quicken.

Riding over to the schoolhouse, he rehearsed exactly what he was going to say, passing a group of energetic children scurrying home to complete their homework for the next day.

The schoolyard was empty except for one solitary horse, who stood patiently waiting for its owner. Max tied his own horse next to the other and slowly approached the small building. Removing his hat, fixing his hair, and clearing his throat, he walked inside.

At the front of the classroom sat a large desk with a single occupant, meticulously working with a pile of papers on one side and a stack of books on the other. Max swallowed hard. His palms grew sweaty. Taking a deep breath, he walked closer to the desk until he was just feet away.

Max stood still for a moment, his presence unknown by the schoolteacher. For a moment, he considered just turning around and walking out. After all, he was an outlaw, unworthy of anyone's love and affection. Katelyn deserved better.

Yet in the silence of the small schoolhouse came Max's answer, ringing loud and clear. His past was behind him. He now had a chance to truly set things straight, to become the man he wanted to be. He loved Katelyn, and he knew that those many years ago when they were both young and happy, she had loved him. If she had cared for him once, surely she could find it in her heart to do so again.

Gathering all the courage and optimism he could muster, Max straightened his shoulders and said the first words that came to mind.

"Excuse me."

Katelyn jumped and let out an "oh!" in surprise.

"Oh, I'm sorry. I didn't mean to scare you."

Regaining her composure, Katelyn chuckled.

"No, it's alright," she reassured him. "I didn't hear you walk in."

"I should have knocked. I'm sorry."

"Don't be."

The two stared at each other awkwardly for a moment, and then a realization suddenly struck Katelyn.

"Wait! Aren't you the man I saw in the mercantile yesterday?"

"Yes ma'am," Max replied.

Katelyn paused, looking at Max's features more closely.

"It's funny. You look so familiar. Have we met before?"

"A long time ago." Max's voice was filled with emotion, and Katelyn detected it. "We used to be friends," he said, wishing he could refer to their relationship as more than just mere friendship.

Suddenly, Katelyn knew who stood before her. Her eyes widened, and her heart beat with excitement.

"Max?" she gasped.

When he nodded his response, Katelyn put her hand to her mouth and let out a short laugh for joy. She was in complete awe, unsure of just what to say.

"Max Wilson? I can't believe you're here."

"You and me both."

Katelyn shook her head in disbelief and wonder.

"It's been so long," she whispered.

"Too long. That's why I've come to ask if you'd, um, well you see—" Max's speech completely left him, and he stood there stuttering over his words. "I should know this. I rehearsed it fifty times!"

Katelyn giggled and smiled, which gave Max a boost of confidence. Recovering his senses, he said, "I was wondering if you'd like to join me for lunch on Saturday. Then we could have a chance to catch up."

Blushing modestly, Katelyn replied, "I'd love to."

Max could not hide his joy, and an enormous smile swept across his face.

"One o'clock at the hotel?" he asked.

"Sounds good to me."

"Alright, well, um, I'll see you, uh, on Saturday then, and uh—" Max accidentally bumped into one of the desks behind him and spun around to steady it. Katelyn tried to suppress a laugh so as not to embarrass him, but Max was too overjoyed to be embarrassed.

"So, um…yah! I'll see you then!"

"See you then."

Setting his hat square on his head and tipping it politely, Max exited the building. Once he was outside, he added a small skip to his walk and let out a quiet "yahoo" over his success. It had gone much better than he had anticipated, and for the first time in years, he felt happy. He felt hopeful.

*   *   *

After a fun day at her grandma's, Eliza headed home, fully prepared to apologize to her parents for how she had behaved. She opened the cabin door to find her mother at work preparing supper. With one hand on the soup ladle and the other on her hip, Grace tried to ease the pain in her lower back. The baby inside her made it difficult to do just about everything, even to stand without feeling some level of discomfort.

Upon hearing the door open, she turned to see Eliza lingering in the doorway, with her head hung low. Setting the ladle aside and facing her daughter, she gently probed, "Eliza? Is everything alright?"

"No, Mama," Eliza quietly answered.

"Do you want to talk about it?"

Eliza nodded and took a seat at the kitchen table.

"I was talking with grandma today and I feel so bad. I never meant to—" Eliza stopped, and bit her lower lip, attempting to control her emotions which had lately brought her more harm than good. Grace saw her struggle and spoke for her.

"Eliza, I know this must have been hard for you. But I want you to know that your father and I have always loved you, and we always will. You're a part of our family, Eliza, and nothing anybody says will ever change that."

Just as Grace finished speaking, a searing pain shot through her abdomen, and she hurled over, grasping the table for support. Eliza jumped out of her chair and put her arm around her mother's waist to stable her.

"I'm fine, Eliza," Grace assured her, trying to stand upright, though she could not.

"What's wrong, Mama? What is it?"

Through deep, strained breaths, Grace said, "I think the baby might be ready."

"What do you want me to do?" Eliza panicked.

"Help me to my bed!" Another pain pierced Grace, and she was barely able to walk from the kitchen to her room. Situating the pillows just right, Eliza helped her mother lay back. Grace's palm was hot and perspiring, and she clenched Eliza's hand.

"Go get your father!"

Racing out of the cabin, Eliza scurried into the barn where David was feeding the animals.

"Come quick! It's Mama!"

Dropping the bucket of oats, David rushed to his wife. She was soaked with sweat, and trying hard to remain calm.

"David," she pleaded, grasping his arm. He wrapped his large hands around her small, frail ones, and consoled, "It's alright, Grace. I'm here. Eliza, take the wagon and fetch Doctor Martin."

Before David had even finished speaking, Eliza was out of the room. She jumped in the wagon and whipped the reigns. The horses took off, and Eliza pushed them to go faster.

"Hey, look!" Daniel exclaimed when he saw the speeding wagon.

"It's Eliza!" Margaret said.

Eliza flew by her siblings and the Koch children, who were walking home from school.

"Eliza, where are you going?" Aaron shouted after her.

"The baby's coming!" was her hurried response, and within a moment, she was out of sight.

"Hey! Mama's having the baby!" Daniel proclaimed, and

he took off towards home as fast as his short legs could carry him with Ellie following suit.

"Come on! Let's go!" Margaret yanked Aaron's arm in the direction of their cabin, and the three of them raced to tell their mother the news.

"Mama! Mama! Aunt Grace is having the baby!" Margaret yelled, startling Anna, who was preparing supper.

"You scared me, Margaret!" Then, it dawned on her. "Wait! Grace is having the baby...*now*? Oh, dear! Okay, um, Margaret, the chicken is in the oven; it's just about done. I need you to take care of that for me. Samuel, mind your brother and behave yourself now. If your father asks where I am, tell him I'm at the Carvers." Anna swung her shawl over her shoulders and was gone in a flash.

Samuel looked up at Aaron with wide eyes and said, "Babies sure make everybody act crazy, don't they?"

Laughing at his brother's innocence, Aaron rustled his hair and responded, "They sure do, Samuel."

When Anna arrived at the Carvers', she found David pacing in the kitchen and the children seated at the table with nervous expressions. Inside the bedroom, Grace was moaning and shouting from the pain.

"Anna," David said, taking her hand. "Grace will be glad you're here."

"Why don't you take the children out to the barn?" Anna suggested in a hushed voice, not wanting them to worry. "I'll let you know when it's over."

With that, Anna opened the bedroom door and knelt down beside Grace. Mrs. Johnson nodded at her and smiled, silently thanking her for being there. Doctor Martin positioned himself at the end of the bed.

"Alright, Grace, here we go."

                              *   *   *

Dusk slowly faded away, and all turned to darkness. The stars shone brightly above the cabin, and the glimmering moon illuminated the countryside. Everything was peaceful. The yelling had ceased, and the cabin had fallen to silence.

Inside the barn, David paced back and forth. Samuel sighed. Ellie tapped. Eliza worried. All of them prayed. Just when they thought they couldn't stand the wait any longer, Anna emerged and invited them inside.

"How is she?" David asked.

"She's just fine, and so is the baby," Anna replied, placing a comforting hand on David's arm.

"Thank you God."

David and the children stood in the doorway, and Grace glanced up at them with a beautiful yet tired smile.

"You can come in now," she whispered.

David walked over to his wife, and the children huddled around the bed.

"It's a girl," Grace announced, and David looked with pride at his baby daughter.

"She's perfect," he said.

"Can I hold her, Mama?" Ellie asked excitedly.

Grace nodded and tenderly handed the baby to Ellie, who placed a kiss on her tiny forehead.

"Do you have a name?" Mrs. Johnson asked.

Turning to face her mother, Grace replied, "Rebekah Joy, after her aunt."

Those words took Mrs. Johnson by complete surprise, and reopened a wound that had been closed long ago. Her eyes filled with tears as she was reminded of her daughter who had never reached adulthood. She had never lived to see Grace marry, though it was something she had hoped for, and she had never lived to see her nieces and nephews, whom she would have loved so much. Remembering Rebekah's joy and innocence made Mrs. Johnson smile though her heart ached for her daughter to be there, sharing this precious memory.

"She would have been so happy," she told Grace, who knew it to be true.

"She looks like you, Mama!" Daniel exclaimed and slowly reached up to stroke Rebekah's smooth head.

"I think it's the hair," David joked and everyone laughed, though they tried to do it quietly so they wouldn't frighten the little one.

As they all rejoiced in Rebekah's birth, Eliza once again felt out of place. She saw the delight in her mother's eyes and the pride in her father's smile. This was their child, their flesh and blood, a testament to their great love for each other. Gazing at Rebekah's fair skin and blue eyes, Eliza was reminded of the fact that she would never look like her family. She would forever, and only, be adopted.

CHAPTER FIFTEEN

A SEED OF TRUTH

Saturday came, though not quickly enough for Max, who had spent the past three days worrying over, while at the same time, anticipating his next meeting with Katelyn. The first one had gone much better than he had dreamed it could, and this encouraged him, though it did not completely calm his nerves.

As he stood in front of the mirror adjusting his hair for the hundredth time, Jake came in, surprised to see his brother fussing with his appearance.

"What are you doing?" he asked gruffly.

"Combing my hair."

"I can see that," Jake snipped back. "*Why* are you combing your hair?"

Max hesitated for a moment, afraid of the ridicule he was sure to receive once he told his brother about Katelyn.

"I'm meeting someone for lunch," was his reply, hoping Jake wouldn't ask any more questions.

Jake looked at his brother for a moment and then smiled knowingly.

"A lady friend?" he teased.

"Actually, yes," Max answered shortly, tired of his brother's mockery and ridicule. After all, Max was a grown man. He was free to make his own decisions without his brother's supervision. Or was he?

"I spoke with Katelyn the other day. She's meeting me at the hotel at one o'clock."

"What? You've got to be joking!"

"No, I'm not, and I don't see what's so funny about it."

"Oh, please! You can't possibly think that this could go anywhere, Max? What on earth are you trying to prove?"

With a fiery glare in his eyes, Max stared solemnly at Jake.

"I'm not trying to *prove* anything, Jake," he declared. "I'm trying to do things the right way, the way they should have been done a long time ago. And I'd appreciate it if you'd just let me do this without any interference."

Taking a step closer to his brother, Jake smiled and tried to laugh off the seriousness of the moment.

"Listen, Max," he said. "I don't mind you seeing Katelyn, but don't get your hopes up."

"I have to go," Max said and walked past his brother towards the door. Jake, however, wasn't finished.

"Remember who you are, Max, and what we're here to do."

How could Max forget? Jake was a constant reminder of his past and the dark shadow he could never escape.

Without saying another word to his brother, he left the room.

"Where are you off to?" Henry asked as Max came down the stairs.

"To the hotel. I'm meeting someone for lunch."

"Really? Who is it?"

"Uh…" Max hesitated. Would Henry mock him, too? "Miss Barton, the schoolteacher."

"Oh," Henry responded with a genuine smile. "Well, have a good time!"

Henry's reply took Max by surprise. He was actually nice to him.

"Thanks. I'm sure I will."

As Max mounted his horse and rode into town, he thought of the stark contrast between Jake and Henry. Jake, who had never said a kind word to Max in his life, was the one he had followed since childhood, the one who had convinced him to run away and leave everything and everyone he had ever loved.

Henry, on the other hand, had received them back with kindness. He wasn't overpowering or rude. Max felt loved and respected when he was around him. Yet this was the man he had come back to get rid of, and why?

Jake should have inherited the plantation, but their father had planned to give it to Henry, the youngest, when he saw the discontentment and bitterness that plagued Jake's heart and the irresponsibility that defined Max's character. For this, Jake had carried a grudge for the past two decades, allowing bitterness to take root and poison his mind. He had always wanted more as a boy…more power, more wealth and now he had achieved that through his criminal ways. But it still wasn't enough, and it never would be.

Max felt conflicted. He had been loyal to Jake all these years. But now he was seeing the consequences of his choices. Jake had taken advantage of him and would continue to use him for his evil purposes as long as he lived. The only one who had ever shown him any love over these past twenty years was Henry, and if Jake had his way, he'd be dead within a month.

Max had wanted a change, a fresh start, and he finally now had a chance at one. He wasn't going to let Jake stop that.

*   *   *

Eliza stood over the cradle, looking down at her baby sister, who was sleeping peacefully. These past three days had brought a lot of change. Grace's focus had been shifted to tending to Rebekah's every need, day and night. No one had gotten a full night's rest or even close to it, and they were all exhausted. Eliza had her hands full between doing chores, helping her mother, and taking care of Rebekah. Mrs. Johnson and Anna stopped by each day to see how things were going and help in what way they could, but Eliza took on most of the responsibilities since she was the oldest child.

Even though she was worn out from the work, it was hard for her to be angry as she gazed at the sweet baby before her. However, she could not help envying Rebekah.

"You know," she whispered, "you're really blessed to have a family that loves you so much."

Eliza envied all the attention Rebekah was getting. She envied her complete ignorance of the world and all of its troubles. Most of all, she envied how Rebekah would never have to experience the shame and prejudice that came with being black.

No white person could ever love a Negro! She's not like us! She doesn't belong here…and she never will.

Those words kept ringing in Eliza's mind. She tried to silence them, but they only came back louder and stronger.

You only give your family a bad name.

These were the most painful of all. The last thing she wanted was to bring shame to her family, but it seemed that this was all she had ever done.

Right then and there, Eliza knew what she had to do.

*   *   *

At the hotel, Max and Katelyn were enjoying their lunch. The years faded away as they talked, laughed, and reminisced of old times. Max shared what he could of his story with Katelyn, and she was fascinated with the places he had gone. He wished he didn't have to conceal anything from her, yet he knew that she would probably never speak with him again if she was aware of even half the things he had done.

Katelyn, Max learned, was an only child and had spent the last several years of her life alone since her parents had died from the fever. She loved teaching and said that it provided her with well-needed company and distraction from the loneliness she felt at home.

After a slight lull in the conversation, Max shifted topics to a more personal matter.

"Katelyn," he softly began. "I know we don't know each other very well and that it's been a while since we were friends. But I was hoping that we could get to know each other better and well…" Max paused. He knew how he felt, but he struggled to put it into words.

"Yes?" Katelyn invited him to continue.

"Katelyn," he tenderly pleaded. "I'd like to be your beau."

Max's frankness took Katelyn off guard. She knew he cared for her, but she hadn't expected him to express it this early in their relationship.

"Oh," she replied, raising her napkin to wipe the corners of her mouth.

"I know it's soon, and I'm willing to wait if you need more time, but—"

"No, it's not that," Katelyn interrupted. "It's just…"

"What?"

Katelyn contemplated what to say so as not to offend Max. She did care for him—she had since she was a little girl—but he was a grown man now, different from the child she had once known. A question burdened her mind, and she knew Max's answer would determine whether or not their relationship could continue.

"I need to ask you something, Max," she continued. "Are you a Christian?"

Max sat back in his chair and sighed.

"I haven't stepped foot in a church for a very long time if that's what you mean."

He tried to justify his actions with "Jake and I were constantly moving from place to place, so there wasn't much time for church. Most of the towns we came across didn't even have one."

"Well, do you own a Bible?"

"No. I was never a big reader." Although he said it with a smile and a chuckle, he knew to Katelyn it was not a joking matter.

Katelyn was disappointed to say the least. She desperately wanted to continue seeing Max, but her conscience told her otherwise. She couldn't allow her feelings to stand in the way of her faith.

"I see," Katelyn responded. "I'm not trying to pry or anything, but ever since I was a little girl, I've known that *if* I were to marry someday, I could only marry someone who shares my beliefs."

"I understand. I just don't know if I—" Max chose not to say anymore. Telling Katelyn to her face that he thought religion was for the weak and the Bible a mere book of fairy tales would only make her distance herself more from him.

There was an awkward silence, and after a moment, Katelyn rose from the table to leave. If Max was not saved, there was no point in prolonging the inevitable.

"Well, thank you for lunch," she said with a sad smile.

"Thank you for coming."

Katelyn left the restaurant feeling more dejected and lonely than normal. However, she knew she had done the right thing.

Max took his time riding home, reflecting on their conversation. He felt defeated and frustrated and scolded himself over and over again for his faulty response.

Nice, Max! You could have at least made her think you were somewhat interested! Now she'll probably never speak to you again.

When he arrived back home, he saw Jake once again engaged in his shooting lessons with Robert and James.

"How'd it go?" Jake called out to his brother.

Choosing to ignore him, Max tied his horse up and walked inside.

"What's the matter with him?" Robert asked his uncle.

"He didn't take my advice, and now he's suffering the consequences," Jake stated nonchalantly. "Come on. Let's keep practicing."

Max spent that night tossing and turning, agonizing over his past mistakes. How could he have been so foolish? He couldn't let Katelyn go that easily. He cared too much about her and had wasted enough time already. There was only one thing he could do if he wanted to earn Katelyn's trust.

The next morning, he rose and dressed himself. Tucking the edges of his shirt in neatly and straightening the collar, he once again stood in front of the mirror, fixing himself. He took the wash basin on the nightstand, wet his hair, and brushed it to the side.

When he joined the rest of the family for breakfast, Lillian was the first to speak to him.

"You're looking nice this morning, Max," she complimented. "Are you going somewhere?"

"As a matter of fact, I am." Glancing at his brother, who had one eyebrow raised in a questioning, disapproving manner, he stated, "I'm going to church."

Everyone stopped eating, and Jake cleared his throat slowly. Max knew that was his way of expressing his disapproval.

"This doesn't have anything to do with Miss Barton, does it?" Henry inquired with a grin.

"Yes, it does," he answered, taking a sip of his coffee.

Robert and James exchanged boyish smirks.

"Are you sweet on Miss Barton?"

"Boys," Henry rebuked. "Mind your manners."

As the family continued eating their meal, Jake didn't say a word, which meant he would have plenty to say on the subject later when he and Max were alone.

The service had just begun when Max arrived. As quietly as possible, he opened the door and took a seat in one of the back pews. That's when he saw her. Katelyn was seated in the pew across from him. Turning to see who the newcomer was, Katelyn met Max's gaze. His heart soared when she smiled kindly at him, and he knew he had pleased her by coming.

As the sermon progressed, Max's focus began to shift from Katelyn to the words being preached. He couldn't explain it, but something was stirring inside of him. As the Word of God was declared, Max felt that maybe there was something more to this faith than he had thought. Maybe, just maybe, there was some truth to it.

After the sermon, Katelyn approached him, and with the sweetest voice Max had ever heard, she said, "I'm glad you came."

"So am I," he responded, and he wasn't just referring to Katelyn. "He's a good preacher."

"Yes, he is." Katelyn hesitated for a minute and then asked, "Maybe you'd like to join me again next Sunday?"

"I'd love to. And maybe you'd like to join *me* again for lunch at the hotel on Saturday."

"I'd like that."

Max left the service that day not only encouraged but challenged. He knew he had done the right thing by coming, not just because it had pleased Katelyn, but because his heart had been awakened to truth it had not heard since he was a child. While he wasn't yet fully convinced, a seed had been planted in his soul.

All it needed was time to grow.

CHAPTER SIXTEEN

FOUND OUT

Over the next few weeks, Katelyn and Max grew closer together. Max continued to attend church, and after each time, he felt restored. He knew he could lead a new life, a right life. Not only was he full of confidence, but he was also starting to soften. Katelyn had truly impacted his life for the better. She prayed for him daily, and she could already see the fruit of her faithfulness. She was open about her beliefs when Max asked her questions, and she could tell he was deeply pondering her words. The seed in his heart was being watered.

While Max and Katelyn's relationship was being strengthened, Eliza was distancing herself more from her family and friends. She did her tasks without complaining, and she smiled when others came around, but inside, she was still deeply hurting. She would play a game of hide-n-seek on occasion to make her siblings and friends happy, but she was far from being her normal self. The ongoing struggle inside of her made it impossible to be content with her present circumstances, and she was miserable. Eliza was ignoring the only One who could bring her total peace. She was fighting against His will and was simultaneously fighting against her only chance to be filled with joy. Until she fully submitted to Him, she would never be content or truly joyful.

Friday night rolled around and Max sat down on his bed with a sigh, exhausted from a hard day's work. His back and feet were aching, and he could not wait to kick off his boots and lay his head on his pillow. But Jake had other plans for their evening.

"We need to talk," he demanded.

"About what?" Max asked, rubbing his left foot.

"What do you think? About Katelyn, about church, about everything!"

"I don't see why you're making such a big deal out of this, Jake."

"Max, I didn't come this far just to have you mess it all up now!"

"I don't know what you mean."

"You know exactly what I mean!" Jake sneered. "I've seen the change in you. This church nonsense is messin' with your mind. You're not *thinking* straight anymore. You've become weak and vulnerable!"

Leaning on the bedpost, Jake bent in closer.

"I've seen what you're capable of Max. Have you forgotten everything we've done together? Everything we've gone through to get where we are right now? We can't afford any mistakes. I'm not going back to prison. You understand me?"

Max didn't want to comply, but what choice did he have? He reluctantly nodded his head.

"Good." Jake's mood instantly switched, and he acted like nothing had happened. "I promised Robert and James we'd go hunting tomorrow. You wanna come?"

"Sure."

As the light was extinguished and the brothers were surrounded by darkness, they were unaware that their conversation had not been private.

In the morning they awoke and had just finished dressing when someone knocked on their door. Jake answered it to find Henry standing there, his face solemn.

"Good morning Henry!" Jake greeted him with a smile.

"I'll be frank, Jake," Henry said. As much as it hurt him, he knew what he had to do. "You and Max need to leave."

"What?!?" Jake asked with a laugh. "What do you mean?"

"Don't play innocent with me. I overheard your conversation last night. I'm very disappointed to say the least. It pains me to do this, but I can't have criminals under my roof...not even if they're my brothers."

Jake was doing an excellent job cloaking his anger, but Max's grief was evident. They had been fools to think their past wouldn't catch up with them.

"I want you out before sunup tomorrow. If you're not, I'll have to bring in the sheriff," Henry stated, even though his heart was aching. He didn't want his family to be separated again.

"I won't say anything to the boys," he reassured them, still wanting their reputation to be protected. "They'll be heartbroken enough as it is. They really looked up to you."

Jake could only nod in response.

Hanging his head in dismay, Henry whispered in agony, "I didn't want it to be this way, but I have no choice. I'm sorry."

As Henry walked away, Jake closed the door and clenched his teeth. His plans had been foiled, but he was *going* to get his revenge.

*   *   *

Eliza stood in the kitchen, helping her mother and Ellie make cookies for the event the next day. The Johnsons were hosting a party to celebrate Rebekah's birth. They had done the same thing for all of the Carver children, and everyone was anticipating the special day.

"I can't believe she's almost a month old already!" Ellie exclaimed. "Time goes so fast."

"That's for sure," Grace said. "I can still remember when both of you were babies, lying in that same cradle. Your father made it for you, Eliza. Did you know that?"

"No," Eliza responded, glancing at the spot where Rebekah lay, cooing contentedly.

"He was so proud of himself and so happy," Grace reminisced. "See, until we had you, Ellie, we were unable to have children. Your father and I prayed and prayed. Just when I had almost given up hope, the Lord brought Eliza into our lives."

Eliza looked at her mother, who was smiling kindly.

"You were everything we had ever hoped for in a child. You were healthy and happy and funny. You should have seen the faces she used to make." Grace laughed as she recounted all the joyous times she had when Eliza was younger.

"Nothing's changed!" Ellie teased, nudging her sister.

"Very funny," Eliza said, and she couldn't help but chuckle.

"The Lord definitely knew what He was doing when He made you our daughter," Grace told Eliza. "He knew we needed you."

You don't need me, Eliza thought. *Everything will be better for everyone once I'm gone.*

Grace and the girls continued baking, and their conversation was filled with light-hearted recollections of when the girls were babies. Though it should have brought her joy, the stories of her childhood only made Eliza's heart heavier. Those days were gone. Things were not the way they once had been long ago nor would they ever be again.

As the light of day vanished and was replaced by night, Jake and Max packed their things to leave. Their last day at the plantation had been spent entertaining the boys. Robert and James had grown quite good with handling guns thanks to the training Jake had given them. They begged him to take them hunting so they could show off what they'd learned. Jake didn't tell them that he and Max were leaving. He didn't want to explain. He knew the boys would be sad, but quite honestly, he didn't care. He was too upset over his own loss.

Max was devastated. Not only was he leaving his family, he was leaving Katelyn without even being able to say goodbye.

Just as dawn broke, the brothers had their things packed and were mounting their horses to leave. Gazing one last time at the place he had called home, Max rode away as he had done so many years before, refusing to look back.

The brothers were silent for a long while, riding farther away from the plantation and deeper into the woods. Not a creature stirred. No wind blew. The trees loomed above them, blocking out the light.

"Man," Max sighed, glancing around at the dreariness that enveloped them. "We really blew it this time. If only we had —"

"Would you shut up? I'm trying to think!" Jake fumed. It was the first time he had spoken since they had left the plantation.

When he grew restless from sitting on his horse, Jake yanked the reigns back and jumped down. For several minutes, he walked alone, stomping his boots into the soft dirt beneath him and kicking the plants in his path. Shaking his fists, he let out a wrathful cry at the top of his lungs, one that sent shivers down Max's spine.

Punching the ground in fury, Jake breathed heavy, vengeful breaths. Suddenly, he saw something in the distance. It looked to be a shack of some sort. He slowly raised himself up and walked toward the gloomy hut. Cobwebs entangled him as he stepped inside, and he aggressively pushed his way through. There was nothing, except an unshakable, eerie silence.

Barely any light shone through the door, but it was just enough to reveal three letters that had been hastily painted on the wall: KKK. Evil work had been done there, and it filled Jake with hellish pleasure.

"Max!" he boomed. "Get over here!"

Rolling his eyes, Max led the horses over to the spot where Jake was.

"What is it?"

Emerging from the shadows, Jake stood before his brother, and Max sensed a great evil had overcome him. His eyes had become blackened with hate, and any sense he may have once had was gone.

He was possessed.

"We're going back," he announced.

"What do you mean? There's nothing for us there now."

"That's where you're wrong. Tell me," he snarled, "what does Henry value most? It's not his plantation."

"No, it would be—" Max stopped as he realized what his brother planned to do. A demonic grin crept across Jake's face.

"Jake…you can't! You can't possibly—"

"Robert and James are the key to Henry's undoing. We'll

take them hostage and hold them for ransom. If Henry doesn't pay what we demand, we'll kill the boys."

"That's absurd!"

"Is it?" Jake shot back. "Henry took everything away from us. Now we're just returning the favor. I'm not gonna let two brats get my inheritance."

"I won't go through with this, Jake! You can't make me!"

Snatching his pistol from its holster, Jake aimed it directly at his brother.

"If you fail me now," he hissed, "you won't live to regret it."

Swallowing hard, Max's jaw tightened in rage. He hated being his brother's pawn, but he had no choice. His death meant nothing. Jake would do his dirty work with or without his help. Once again, Max reluctantly nodded in compliance.

"I thought so," Jake sneered. "Now come on!"

* * *

Back at the plantation, the Wilsons sat around the table, silently eating their breakfast until Robert broke the silence.

"It's not fair!" he declared. "Why did they have to leave?"

"I told you already, Robert," Henry explained. "Something came up. They didn't want to leave, but they had to."

"It doesn't make any sense."

"We were gonna go fishing today, too," James sighed.

"You boys can still go fishing," Lillian tried to cheer them up.

"It was always more fun with them."

"You can still have a good time. Why don't you go after breakfast? It will help take your mind off of things."

Once they finished their meal, the boys grabbed their poles and headed to the secluded spot where they had so often fished with their uncles. They sat for a while, casting and recasting their lines but with no luck.

Suddenly, they heard footsteps behind them. They slowly turned around not knowing what to expect, but upon seeing who the visitor was, they jumped to their feet in excitement.

"Uncle Jake! You're back!" the boys exclaimed simultaneously.

"Hello, boys! How are you doing?"

"A lot better now!" Robert beamed.

"We were so sad when our pa told us you had to leave."

"Yah, I didn't want to, but that's life. You have to do lots of things you don't always want to do."

"Then, you're still leaving?" Robert asked.

"I have to Robert," Jake faked his sadness. "But before I leave, I thought we could get one last round of fishing in. Does that sound good?"

"Yah! Maybe now that you're here we'll actually catch something!"

"As a matter of fact, I found an even better spot where the fish are bitin' like crazy!"

"Really?"

"You betcha! Come on. It's only a short ways away."

CHAPTER SEVENTEEN

CAPTIVE

After church, the Carvers went back home before heading over to the Johnsons. Grace fed Rebekah, and Daniel begged to change into his more comfortable clothes.

"Alright, Daniel," Grace consented. "But I want you to fold that shirt and put it away *neatly*. Do you understand?"

"Yes, ma'am."

Eliza knew that the time had come to do what she had been planning for weeks.

"Mama?"

"Yes, Eliza?"

"I don't feel well. My stomach's been bothering me, and I feel a little sick. I don't think I should go to the party."

"You don't have a fever, do you?" Grace asked, putting her hand to Eliza's forehead.

"No."

"What's the matter?" David queried upon overhearing some of their conversation.

"Eliza's not feeling well."

"Are you alright?"

"I'm fine. It's just my stomach. I think I just need some rest."

"Alright, but if you feel better, come over and join us."

"Okay."

David leaned down and kissed his daughter's forehead.

They gathered the baked treats from the previous day and prepared to leave. Grace turned to her daughter.

"Get some sleep."

"I will."

Eliza watched her family get in the wagon and ride away. When she was sure they were gone, she took a piece of paper and a pencil and wrote a short note. Then, shoving a few pairs of clothes and some food in her mother's carpetbag, she left the cabin, closing the door behind her.

She walked for a good half hour, passing many familiar spots: the stream where she had so often found solace, the large pine tree, under whose mighty branches she had cried for comfort. After a long while, she decided to sit on a large rock in the woods to take a rest. She took a piece of bread out of her bag, trying to rejuvenate her strength.

"I have to keep going. It'll be better for everyone," she kept telling herself, but the farther away from home she got, the lonelier she became.

*   *   *

"You tricked us!"

Robert and James sat up against the wall of the shack with their uncle's gun posing an imminent threat on their life.

"Don't take it too hard, boys. It's nothing personal," Jake answered with a smirk. "Tie em' up, Max."

Max had no option but to obey his brother.

"I'm sorry, boys," he said. "I wish it didn't have to be this way."

As his hands were bound, Robert looked pleadingly into his uncle's eyes.

"Why? Why are you doing this Uncle Jake?"

"I've got a score to settle with your father."

"What did he ever do to you?"

Kneeling down so he was eye-level with Robert, Jake snarled, "He ruined my life. He took away everything that should have been mine." After both boys' hands were tied, Jake raised himself back up to his full height, and his nephews became afraid.

"This revenge is long overdue. One way or another, I will get what I want."

Just then, a shout was heard outside the shack, startling everyone. Jake took a step closer to the door.

"Watch them," he ordered and carefully walked outside.

He slowly scanned his surroundings. He saw nothing, but he was positive someone was out there. Walking a short distance away from the shack, he spotted movement in the brush.

"Well, well, well. What do we have here?" Yanking his victim to her feet, he dragged her inside the shack. The boys' jaws dropped when they saw who it was.

"Eliza?!?" Robert exclaimed.

"Well, well, well." Jake smiled. "Do you two know each other?"

"What are you doing here?" he queried.

"Running away it would seem," Jake stated, shoving Eliza to the floor and tossing her carpetbag to the side. "Tie her up, Max. We can't have anyone giving away our hiding place, now can we?"

*   *   *

As the clock struck five, Lillian paced in the parlor, and Henry sat on the sofa reading the paper.

"They should have been home by now," Lillian worried.

"I'm sure they're fine, dear. Knowing our boys, they probably went fishing for a while, got bored, and found something else to do. This isn't the first time they've been late coming home. Those boys have no respect for rules."

"Do you think that's all it is?"

"I'm positive."

Resuming her needlepoint, Lillian tried to take her mind off of her missing boys and convince herself that it was truly just an oversight on their part or a disregard for the rules like Henry said.

Simultaneously, the party at the Johnsons had just come to a close, and the Carvers and Kochs were on their way home. It had been a wonderful day filled with delicious food and precious memories made with dear friends. No one knew the heartache that evening would bring.

When they arrived back at their cabin, Grace told Ellie and Daniel to keep their voices down so as not to disturb Eliza if she were sleeping. They obeyed, and everyone entered the cabin quietly. Grace took Rebekah into their bedroom and laid her in her cradle.

"You were a very good girl today," she said. "Everyone loves you so much."

Just as Grace was wrapping Rebekah in her blanket, she heard Ellie shout, "Mama! Mama!"

"What is it, Ellie?" Grace asked, frightened.

"Eliza's gone!" she exclaimed.

"What?"

"I found this note on her bed."

Taking the note from her daughter, Grace called frantically to her husband.

"David, Eliza's run away! Here, read this."

David read the note and took a deep breath.

"Dear Lord, help us!" he begged. "Grace, stay here with Ellie and Rebekah. Daniel, I need you to go get your grandpa and grandma and bring them here quickly. I'll get the Kochs."

David took his wife's hands in his.

"Look at me. Everything will be fine. We're gonna find her."

As soon as everyone was assembled at the Carvers', David gave directions.

"Grace and I will head north. Jonathan and Anna, you head south, and Mr. and Mrs. Johnson you go east. We'll meet back here in an hour."

"We can help, too!" all the children offered.

"I need at least one of you to stay with Rebekah. Daniel and Samuel, I'd feel better if you stayed, too," David said.

"I can stay with them," Margaret offered.

"Alright. Aaron and Ellie, you head east. Is everyone clear?"

Everyone agreed, and with that, they went their separate ways.

Spanning far and wide, they searched for Eliza, calling her name countless times and praying for guidance. Grace tried desperately to keep calm, but not knowing if her child was dead or alive frightened her more than anything else ever had.

Just when it seemed like it could not get any worse, thunder crashed in the sky above. Rain was coming.

"Aaron," Ellie said, resting her hand on her knees. "Hold on. I need to catch my breath."

"Yah, me, too."

Aaron looked at Ellie, and he could tell she was trying not to cry.

"Do you think we'll find her?" she asked.

Aaron wanted to stay positive, but right now, he was feeling hopeless. Only the Lord knew where Eliza was, and only He could open their eyes to find her.

Reaching for Ellie's hands, Aaron prayed, "Lord, we need Your help. We're tired, and we're scared. Please help us to find her. Please Lord." This was more than just a request. It was an earnest plea, a cry to the only One who could hear them and come to their aid.

"Let's keep going," Aaron said, but Ellie's hand gripped his arm. That's when he saw it: a light blue hair ribbon. The two friends looked at each other in disbelief.

"She was here," Ellie said. She was just getting ready to shout Eliza's name when Aaron's hand covered her mouth.

"Shhh," he whispered. "Look."

In the distance stood two horses, grazing, and just beyond them, a shack.

"Do you think Eliza's in there?" Ellie wondered.

"I don't know, but I have a bad feeling. Stay close."

As the two crept closer to the shack, they made sure to avoid any twigs or other noisy items that could give them away. They looked inside through one of the tiny cracks in the wall. All they could see were the backs of two large figures, facing the opposite wall.

"It'll be dark soon," they heard one of them say.

"I know that!" the other snarled, and he took a step to his right, revealing one of their captives.

Ellie stifled a gasp, and Aaron's jaw dropped.

"What are we gonna' do with her?"

"Why don't we take her with us?" Jake sarcastically snipped. "What do you *think* we're gonna do with her?"

"Only seems reasonable that we'd let her go. She can't do us any harm once we're gone."

That's when Ellie and Aaron saw the two other captives, and their eyes grew wide with shock.

"When it gets dark, I want you to take the note. We'll figure out what to do with her later. We can't let her go now, that's for sure."

The two spies didn't stay around to hear anything else, and when they were far enough away from the shack, they bolted as fast as they could to tell the others of their discovery.

CHAPTER EIGHTEEN

THE RESCUE

"Father! Father!" Ellie shouted as the Carvers' cabin came into view. The Kochs and Carvers were there, but the Johnsons had not yet returned.

"Ellie! There you are! We were starting to worry."

"We found Eliza!" Aaron exclaimed, out of breath.

"What? Where is she? Why didn't you bring her back?" Grace questioned.

"We couldn't. She—"

"She what?"

"She's being held captive."

The four adults let out gasps of horror.

"What are you talking about, Aaron?" Grace's tone was much more frustrated and frantic.

"Well, we found Eliza's light blue hair ribbon in the woods, so we knew she must be close by. That's when Aaron saw two horses and a shack a little ways off. So we went over to see, and there were these two men inside with guns. And...and we saw Eliza. But that's not all. We saw Robert and James, too."

"Robert and James *Wilson*?" Anna asked.

"Yes."

"Did you hear anything, Ellie?" David needed answers.

"We didn't stay for long. They did say something about, about a note."

"A note?"

"A ransom note," David voiced. "They probably know Henry's rich and are holding the boys for ransom." Turning to his friend, he said, "Jonathan, I need you to go get Sheriff Taylor and Henry. Take Aaron with you and meet us there."

"You got it! Aaron, let's go!"

As swiftly as possible, Aaron helped his father detach the horses from the wagon, and David did the same with his team.

"Ellie, I'll need you to come with me," David instructed.

"But it's dangerous," Grace fretted.

"I don't have an option, Grace. Ellie and Aaron are the only ones who know where she is."

Hugging her daughter and husband goodbye, Grace begged, "Be safe, both of you!"

"We will."

David pulled Ellie up on his horse. Before he left, he looked down at his wife and took her hand that was extended to him.

"I'll be praying. We all will," she told him.

"Good. Remember, Grace, she's in His hands. He's watching over her."

"I know."

With a flick of the reigns, David and Ellie took off in the direction of the shack.

*   *   *

As the sun drifted slowly below the horizon, David and Ellie sat in silence. They had left their horse back a distance so the outlaws would not hear them approach. Suddenly, they heard footsteps behind them.

"It's only us," Jonathan whispered. "Anything happening?" asked the sheriff.

"No, we haven't heard a sound since we got here. Aaron, I think it'd be best if you and Ellie went back to the cabin."

"But I want to help," Aaron said.

"No, Aaron, it's too dangerous," Jonathan told his son. "Do as he says."

Even though Aaron longed to stay, he knew he also had to look out for Ellie's safety. Reluctantly, he and Ellie left to retrieve their horse and ride home.

"Alright, men, let's go. But keep quiet and watch your step."

Inside the shack, Eliza sat frozen with fear and a single tear fell down her face.

Why was I so foolish? Why? Now I'll never see my family again.

Seeing her fright, Robert, for the first time, felt convicted for having hurt her.

"Let me see that," Jake ordered and yanked the ransom note out of his brother's hands.

"Good," he said. "Now, I want you take this to the plantation and—"

Just then, a shot was fired outside of the hideout, cutting his sentence short.

"Drop your weapons, and come out with your hands in the air! We've got you surrounded!"

"That sounds like your father," Robert whispered to Eliza, and a small sigh escaped her lips. However, her feeling of relief was not long-lasting. Jake yanked her to her feet with his pistol at her back. His massive hand wrapped around her forearm as he dragged her outside and held her in front of his body, shielding himself from any danger.

"I advise *you* to drop *your* weapons," the thug snarled at

David. "One wrong move…and I'll kill her."

It killed David to see his daughter in the grip of this gruesome man. There was nothing anybody could do to stop him.

Or was there?

"No, Jake."

The voice came from behind the outlaw.

"You're not going to harm that girl…or anyone else here."

Jake chuckled demonically.

"And just what do you think will stop me?" he taunted.

The hammer of Max's pistol clicked behind him.

"There aren't any bullets in that gun Jake."

Jake's face immediately grew tense…and scared. Without releasing Eliza, he pulled the trigger while pointing the gun out in front of him. Nothing happened. He tried two more times, but no bullets were shot.

He had been betrayed.

"It's over, Jake," Max stated firmly. "Let her go."

Gritting his teeth, Jake harshly shoved Eliza to the ground. With a fiery look in his eyes, he spewed, "It's not over yet."

In a flash, Jake spun around and hit the pistol out of Max's hands, causing the gun to fire. Eliza looked up in time, just to see her father fall to the ground.

"Father!" she cried, rushing to his side. The bullet had struck his arm.

An intense fight ensued between Jake and Max. Sheriff Taylor reached for his gun, but Henry stopped him.

"Don't shoot!" he shouted, still wanting his brother's life to be spared. There was no guarantee the sheriff would even hit Jake and not Max.

"You betrayed me!" Jake snarled as he and Max wrestled furiously.

"You left me no choice."

With a shout of fury, Jake lashed at his brother. Max, however, shoved forward with every ounce of strength left in his body. What neither of them saw was the old tree that had fallen behind Jake. Impacted by the blow from Max, Jake tripped backwards over the log, causing Max to fall directly on top of him. When Max went to strike his brother, he realized the fight was over. Underneath Jake's head was a large stone.

It was over.

A sudden relief swept over Max as he sat there for a brief moment stunned, gazing at the man whom he had considered an enemy more than a brother. Jake was no longer a threat to anyone, nor would he ever be again.

The moment was short-lived, however, as Sheriff Taylor held his gun at Max's back.

"Alright, on your feet," he ordered.

Max knew there was no escape this time. He was caught, and he was going to pay. David's cry, however, awoke Max from the daze he was in, and he knew what he had to do.

"I've dealt with these kind of wounds before," he hastily told Sheriff Taylor. "Please, let me help him."

Sheriff Taylor looked from Max to David and then back to Max. His eyes were full of concern, and the sheriff could see his sincerity. Since Max was unarmed and the horses had bolted, he had no way to escape. He was at the mercy of the law now, and the sheriff nodded, permitting him to help.

Max wasted no time. Taking the flask of whiskey from his dead brother's jacket, he hurried over to David and bent down beside him.

"He's fading quickly," Jonathan said, and Eliza sat beside

him, crying and stroking her father's head.

Max opened the flask and poured some of the whiskey on the wound. Taking a knife from his pocket, he handed it to Jonathan.

"Cut some moss off of that tree and bring it here quickly!"

Jonathan did as he was instructed, and Max placed the moss on David's arm. David's breathing was heavy, and he was sweating badly.

"It's alright, Eliza. It's alright," he managed to say, just as his eyes closed, and his head fell limp in her arms.

"Father! No! No, please don't die!" she wept.

"He's not dead," Max reassured her. "He's unconscious."

Cutting a slit in his shirt, Max ripped a long portion off and wrapped it around the moss.

"Don't remove the moss or the cloth," Max directed Jonathan. "If the blood soaks through, just keep adding more layers, and make sure his arm his elevated."

"What about the bullet?" Eliza asked.

"It won't do him any harm where it is. He'll be fine."

Neither Jonathan nor Eliza knew what to say. This man was an outlaw, yet he had just saved David's life. Eliza did not move but Jonathan managed to nod his thanks.

When Max saw his job was done, he stood, knowing what he needed to do next.

"Will you two be alright?" Sheriff Taylor asked.

"Yes," said Jonathan.

"Alright, you," he spoke to Max. "Let's go."

Just as Max turned to leave, he spotted Henry beside the shack with his arms wrapped around his boys. They couldn't speak. They could only stare at Max with shock, anger, and grief overwhelming them.

"I'm so sorry," Max apologized, and it came from a truly repentant heart. "I really am."

When none of them responded, Max walked away with Sheriff Taylor right behind him.

*   *   *

Eliza sat beside her father's bed with his hand in hers. He had been unconscious since the shooting, and Eliza had not left his side.

Several hours had passed since the incident. The original chaos that had occurred when Eliza had returned home was now over. While everyone was relieved to see Eliza, they were all too concerned with David's injury to focus on her. After making sure that David was all right and that his bleeding had stopped, the Kochs and Johnsons returned to their own cabins and Margaret and Daniel were finally able to fall asleep.

Eliza, however, could not sleep. Everything seemed like a blur. She could not wrap her mind around the fact that her father had risked his life to save her...*her*! These past few weeks, she had treated him so badly, yet he had continued to love her. She had run away from home, from the very people who loved her most, yet he had come after her. He nearly died for her.

Kissing his hand and wetting it with her tears, she whispered, "I'm so sorry, Father! This is all my fault. You've always been so good to me, and I've been so awful to you. Please...please forgive me!"

The burden of her sin and selfishness weighed heavy upon Eliza, and she sobbed uncontrollably.

Please forgive me, God! she prayed. *I see now how wrong I've been!*

As she finished her prayer, she felt a gentle hand rub her back. She looked up to see her father's eyes slowly open.

"I forgive you, Eliza."

Hearing those words of forgiveness from her father and seeing that he was alright put Eliza at peace. With tears of joy, she collapsed on her father's chest as he embraced her.

Grace stood at the door, watching the beautiful scene unfold. Her daughter was home, but most importantly, she was healed.

Her prayers had been answered.

CHAPTER NINETEEN

FORGIVEN

The next day, Doctor Martin stopped by to see how David was doing. He inspected and cleaned the wound and gave clear instructions for Grace about how to watch for signs of infection. Because it had already been given proper care, however, he was sure David would be fine and that the wound would heal. This brought tremendous comfort to the family.

Later, the Carvers received a few more visitors.

"Lillian?" Grace asked as she opened the door to find the Wilsons standing there.

"Hello, Grace," Lillian greeted. Though it was not a jovial tone, it was polite.

"Please come in."

Grace didn't know what to make of this. Lillian despised Grace and here she was at her doorstep.

"How is David?" Henry wondered.

"Better. The doctor told us to watch for infection, but he thinks because the wound was treated quickly enough that it'll heal just fine."

"That's good news. Is he up for visitors?"

Motioning to the bedroom, Grace answered, "You can go right in if you'd like."

"Thank you."

When David saw Henry, he tried to sit up.

"Oh, no, please don't," Henry said. Walking closer to the bed and holding his hat in his hands, Henry began, "I want to thank you for everything you did last night. You put your life on the line."

"No thanks is necessary," David replied with a smile. "I just did what any father would have done."

Henry offered his hand, and David shook it. That simple act was the beginning of a new friendship.

In the kitchen, Lillian was having a harder time putting her feelings into words. As full of pride as she was, a twinge of guilt struck her conscience.

"Grace," she started. "First of all, I want to say that I've never been one to admit my faults, particularly because for the longest time, I didn't think I had any."

Grace suppressed a chuckle when she saw how solemn Lillian's countenance had become.

"But last night proved otherwise. It made me realize just how wrong I've been. I wanted to say I'm sorry for how I've treated you and for the things I've said. I was hoping that maybe you could…"

Placing a hand on Lillian's shoulder, Grace replied, "I forgive you, Lillian."

For a moment, Grace was convinced she saw a tear in Lillian's eye.

"Thank you, Grace."

*   *   *

Back at the jail sat a solitary figure with his head in his hands. He was alone, cold, and tired. As he was contemplating everything that had happened, Max heard someone approach.

"Didn't think I'd ever see you again," he said when he recognized his visitor.

"Neither did I," Henry responded. "But things don't always go the way we plan, do they?"

Max was able to chuckle at the statement.

"No," he huffed. "Story of my life."

Henry looked at his brother with compassion. More than anything else, all he wanted was restoration. Now, Jake was dead, and Max was in jail. His heart was broken.

Shaking his head, Max said, "I never wanted things to go the way they did. I came back here fully expecting to lead a different life. But Jake just became so bitter, so vengeful, and I was his slave. He told me what to do, and I did it. I didn't want to, but I did. And now I'm gonna suffer the consequences. I never really wanted to hurt you and your family."

For a moment, nothing could be heard in the jail except for Max's sobs. He cried over his past mistakes, over the things he longed to change but couldn't.

"I won't ask for your forgiveness, Henry. What I did to you and your family…is unforgivable."

At that moment, Henry had a choice to make. He could hold onto the past or he could choose to forgive his brother and do what he could to set his mind at ease. In an act of love, Henry reached through the bars and said, "You're my brother, Max."

Those four words meant more to his troubled soul than anything else could.

*   *   *

Two days passed. David's arm continued to heal, and Eliza was restored to her family and friends. Everything seemed right again.

"Run, Eliza! Go! He's catching up with you!" Margaret squealed as Aaron chased Eliza around the cabin. It was a futile attempt, however, and Aaron eventually caught up and tagged her.

"Ha!" he exclaimed. "That's three points! We win the game!"

Daniel and Samuel exchanged high-fives, and the girls sighed in disappointment.

"I never thought the day would come when I would lose a game of hide-n-seek to *you*, Aaron Koch," Eliza stated.

"Oh, I knew it would come all along!" Aaron boasted.

"Very funny! Hey, you may be faster than me, but I bet I can still beat you at checkers."

"That's for sure!" Ellie proclaimed.

"Well, I don't know about that."

"There's only one way to find out!"

Everyone raced inside to find out who the next checker champion would be!

*   *   *

The day had come for Max to leave. There was one person he longed to see more than anyone else, but she had not come. Unlocking the door to his cell, Sheriff Taylor led Max outside. That's when Max saw her.

"Can we have just a minute…please?" he asked Sheriff Taylor.

"One minute."

As Katelyn approached, Max looked at her sadly. Her face was forlorn, and she held something in her hands.

He didn't have long.

"Katelyn," he started. "I don't even know what to say. You have every right to be angry with me and I'd understand if you—"

"Max," she cut him off. "Henry told me everything."

Max felt sick to his stomach.

"He did?"

Katelyn nodded, but her response was unexpected.

"He told me about your past, but more importantly, he told me what you did to fix it, how you tried to set things right. He told me how you stood up to your brother, and how you saved David Carver's life." Gazing into his eyes, she asked, "How could I be angry with you after that?"

"I lied to you, Katelyn." His tone expressed the agony he was feeling. "I didn't tell you who I really was. I made you think I was a good man, and I'm *not*!"

"Everyone sins, Max, but not everyone has a repentant heart. You do. That guilt you're feeling comes from God. He's reaching out to you, Max, and He has been all along."

"I've done too much in my life for Him to care about me."

"No, Max. It's sinners He came to save. I need His grace just as much as you."

Handing the small item to Max, she said, "Here. I want you to have this."

Max took the gift and stroked the cover.

"Your Bible? No, Katelyn. I can't take this from you." He tried to give it back, but she gently pushed his hand away.

"It's a gift," she told him. "Besides, my father would have wanted you to have it."

"This is your father's Bible?" Max asked, feeling even more honored.

"He read it to me every night when I was younger," she said, smiling as Max flipped through the pages. "It was his most valued possession. After he and mother died, I knew I could only give it to one person."

Placing her hand on his and gazing into his eyes, Katelyn whispered, "To the man I loved."

Max hung his head in shame.

"I had no right to win your heart."

Katelyn raised her hand to Max's cheek and refocused his eyes on her.

"I have never loved any man but you, Max Wilson."

Just as Max was about to speak, Sheriff Taylor announced, "Time to go."

This was the end. Katelyn pressed the Bible into Max's hands and said, "Promise me you'll read it, Max."

"I promise."

Katelyn watched Max until he had completely faded from sight. A tear rolled down her cheek as she wondered whether she would ever see him again.

"You'll always be in my prayers, Max," she whispered to herself.

"Always."

*   *   *

It was late. The sun had set, and the moon had taken its place in the sky. Through her window, Eliza stared in complete awe of its grandeur and radiance.

"I didn't know you were still awake," Grace said as she sat down on the bed beside her daughter.

"Do you see that, Mama?" she asked. "Do you see how *big* it is? How beautiful? And it just sits there."

"What do you mean?" Grace wondered at Eliza's interesting speech.

"I was thinking," Eliza began. "When father got shot, I was so scared. I didn't know what to do or if he'd be okay. But then as I sat there with him the other night, I looked up and saw the moon. And it was like I was finally able to see it clearly."

"What? The moon?"

Eliza turned to face her mother.

"No. *My life.* I mean, I've been struggling for so long, wondering if I truly belonged here. But God finally opened my eyes to show me that I do, that I'm right where I'm meant to be."

Eliza paused, and the joy she was feeling caused her to smile.

"After I ran away," she recounted, "I didn't think I'd ever see you again. But then father found me, and I realized just how much the Lord had done to bring me back home."

"What does the moon have to do with that?" Grace questioned, still not understanding how the two were related.

"As I was caring for father, I thought of something I never had before." Looking out into the starry sky, Eliza said, "The Lord put that moon right there, exactly where He wanted it, so it could give us just the right amount of light we need. And if He's holding that moon in place, controlling it's every move, how much more is He watching over me?"

"That's very wise, Eliza," Grace told her daughter. "The Lord puts His children right where He wants them so they can bring Him the most glory. When we rest in that, He fills us with peace and joy."

Peace and joy, Eliza pondered, and her grandmother's advice came to mind.

"Joy is like a treasure chest, and contentment is the key. Trust that He knows what's best, and be content with what's He's given you, right here, right now, and He will fill you with the joy only He can give."

Eliza now saw the truth in those words. She had learned contentment, and now she was experiencing the peace that surpasses all understanding.

For the first time in her life, she felt true joy.

CHAPTER TWENTY

THE WAR'S END

Max rode a top his horse with the few possessions he had strapped to the saddle. His clothes were dirty, and his hair fanned out in every direction. He was hungry, but he was not empty. He was tired, but he was not defeated. With a smile on his face and a song in his heart, Max pressed his horse to a gallop.

He was finally going home.

Five years had passed since that fateful day when he had been led off to prison, having to leave everything and everyone he loved behind. Max never thought he'd ever see his family and Katelyn again. But in the Lord's providence, he had been given a second chance.

While in prison, Max had read the Bible every day just as he had promised Katelyn, and he was transformed. His eyes were opened to see the man that he was, and the wonderful Savior Jesus is. He was comforted, strengthened, and uplifted. Not only did he read about the Good News of the Gospel, he also shared it with the other prisoners around him, and because of his witness, several of the inmates got saved. For those who were released, they went on to tell others what they had received through Christ, and the hope that they had found. Those who were less fortunate still found joy in their Savior, even as they were being put to death for their crimes.

During those five years of imprisonment, Max read through the Bible multiple times and found more joy in its truth each time he read it. One passage in Colossians brought him tremendous strength, and he meditated on it day and night to comfort him.

"Not that I speak in respect of want: for I have learned, in whatsoever state I am, therewith to be content. I know both how to be abased, and I know how to abound: everywhere and in all things I am instructed both to be full and to be hungry, both to abound and to suffer need. I can do all things through Christ which strengtheneth me."

At first, these verses perplexed Max. How could Paul have been content when he was enduring hunger, shipwreck, imprisonment, and torture? As Max grew to love the Lord and His Word, he realized how this was possible: God's strength and provision. Everywhere that Paul went in life, through every trial he faced, the Lord had been right there beside him. Max was amazed at this. The same God who had been with Paul was now there watching over him in prison. The same Lord who had died to set Paul free from his sins had also given his life for Max's freedom from bondage. Max was no longer a slave to his sin. Jesus had redeemed his soul. This wonderful truth is what brought Max such great joy and what allowed him to view every day as a blessing. Even in prison, Max had learned to be content.

Now, as he was riding home, nothing could dampen his spirit. He didn't know what the future held, but He did know that no matter what happened, His Savior would never abandon him.

After several hours, Max pulled his horse to a halt in front of the schoolhouse like he had done those many years ago. There were no children, no noises, no signs that anyone was still there, except for one horse that stood tied to the fence post.

A flood of doubts suddenly rushed through Max's mind. It had been five years since he had last seen Katelyn. What if she had forgotten him? What if she had fallen in love with someone else?

With his hat in his hands, he offered up a silent prayer.

Lord, I thank You for allowing me to come back home and for watching over me. I know I have no right to ask You for anything else, but please, Lord, grant me this one request: Let me find favor in Katelyn's sight.

Running his hands through his hair and brushing off his dusty jacket, Max tried to make himself presentable. Then, he walked inside.

There at the desk sat Katelyn, exactly as Max had found her five years ago. This time, however, Katelyn heard him enter. Her pencil fell to the desk, and she covered her mouth in shock.

"Max?" she gasped.

"Hello, Katelyn."

Katelyn was speechless. All she could do was run to Max, who swept her up in his arms.

"I've missed you so much!"

"I've missed you, too, Max, more than you know!"

Max reached into his jacket and pulled out the Bible Katelyn had given him.

"I kept my promise," he said. "Before I left, I was still struggling with accepting everything you'd told me about your faith…about this Book." Tears formed in Max's eyes as the magnitude of Jesus' love overcame him. "But the Lord reached down in that damp, dark prison…and He *saved* me, Katelyn! He set me free from my past and gave me peace. Through this

Bible you gave me, He did wonders, not just in my life, but in so many of the other inmates' lives, too."

"Oh, Max!" Katelyn exclaimed, she, too, having begun to cry. "I can't tell you how happy that makes me! I've never stopped praying for you."

"Well, He's answered your prayers. I'm a new man, Katelyn, and this time, I'm going to do things right."

Getting down on his knees, Max took Katelyn's hands in his.

"I know this isn't formal, but I just can't wait any longer." With all the sincerity and love he had to offer, he proposed.

"Katelyn Barton, will you marry me?"

Katelyn's heart soared, and she squealed, "Yes! Of course, I will marry you!"

*   *   *

After his visit with Katelyn, Max knew there was one more stop he had to make. As he approached the plantation, he took a deep breath. Max knew that Henry was not compelled to receive him back. He had opened his door to Max once, but would he do so again?

Max knocked firmly, and a young man, who looked to be about twenty years old, answered. When he recognized the visitor, he asked in unbelief, "Uncle Max?"

"Hello Robert. Is your father here?"

"Yah I'll...I'll go get him."

Robert acted like he had seen a ghost.

"What is it, Robert?" Henry asked as his son entered the parlor.

"Um, there's someone at the door."

Henry rose from his seat and started to walk towards the entrance.

"Who is it?"

Henry did not have to wait long for his answer, for there stood his brother. Lillian, Robert, and James gathered behind him to see what he would do.

Henry and Max stared at each other for a moment, but then, Henry took a step forward and extended his hand.

"Welcome home."

*   *   *

Eliza stood in her room, adjusting the veil on her sister's head.

These past five years had brought much change. Eliza had matured into a beautiful woman, and so had Ellie and Margaret. They found that over the years, their friendship with one another had only been strengthened.

Daniel and Samuel were now teenagers, handsome and head-strong, though still just as interested in adventures as when they were boys. However, they had grown out of their childish ways in that they no longer found pleasure in annoying their siblings, except on a rare occasion here and there when mischief was lacking.

As for Rebekah, she was a healthy, young girl, who adored her older sisters and her straw doll, Clara, whom she had named after her grandma. She regularly convinced Daniel to play dollies with her and was showered with attention from her older siblings and parents.

Aaron was by far the most changed. His voice had deepened, and he had grown to be as tall as his father. He was strong and hard working, and Daniel and Samuel looked up to him.

Over the last year, Aaron had started to develop a closer friendship with Ellie, which slowly turned into something more. After receiving her father's blessing, Aaron proposed. When Eliza heard the news, it did not come as a surprise. She had known Aaron long enough to see that he had started to care for Ellie, and more than anything else, she wanted him to be happy. On occasion, Aaron had asked Eliza for gift ideas to give to Ellie, and it made Eliza happy knowing that his relationship with her sister was budding.

Grace and Anna had always hoped that their children would marry someday, and now that day had come.

"Eliza and Ellie!" Grace called from the kitchen. "Are you almost done?"

"We'll be out in a minute!" Eliza responded, fastening the necklace around Ellie's neck. "There. You're ready."

She stood back admiring her work.

Ellie's hair was curled, and her veil draped softly over her shoulders. The wedding dress, which Grace had given to her, flowed when she walked and glimmered in the light.

"You look so beautiful," Eliza complimented. "I can't wait to see Aaron's face when he sees you. He'll probably faint!"

"Eliza!" Ellie chuckled.

"No, I'm serious Ellie. He will be *stunned*."

"Let me see!" Grace said, bursting into the room. Her patience had run out. "Oh, Ellie." she exclaimed. "You look beautiful."

"Thanks, Mama."

"Mama!" Daniel shouted from the other room. "I can't find my tie!"

"Not again," she murmured to herself. "It should be right in your top dresser drawer."

"I checked, but it's not there."

With a sigh, Grace said, "Hold on. I'll be right there." Turning to her daughters, she chuckled, "When he's thirty, he'll still be asking me where his ties are."

When their mother left the room, Ellie said, "Thank you, Eliza, for everything. I couldn't ask for a better older sister."

"And I couldn't ask for a better younger sister," she smiled, grabbing Ellie's hand. "Well, except for Rebekah."

The two sisters stood there laughing for a moment before Grace re-entered.

"Alright. Let's go," she said. "You can't be late for your own wedding."

The family hopped in the wagon and headed over to the church. When it came time for Ellie to make her entrance, Aaron's heart was filled with pride and a huge smile swept across his face. He was stunned, just as Eliza said he would be.

After the ceremony, everyone stayed to offer their congratulations to the newly-weds before returning home. As Eliza watched Ellie and Aaron, her heart was filled with joy. Her two closest friends were now united as one.

Over the years, Aaron and Ellie's family grew, and Eliza became an aunt to several nieces and nephews, who loved her as much as she loved them.

Though she never married or had children of her own, Eliza was content. She still faced many trials, but through it all, the joy she had found in Christ sustained her until she passed from this life to the next, and the war within her had finally come to an end.

Let the same be true for all of us. Though we face trials and heartaches, let us learn to find our contentment in Christ, for it is only through resting in Him that we will experience perfect peace and joy.

SCRIPTURE REFERENCES

Note from the Author: I added these verses as a help to the reader. They apply to some of the main biblical issues and lessons presented in *The War's End*.

ADOPTION/PREDESTINATION

Psalm 82:3 – Defend the poor and fatherless; do justice to the afflicted and needy.

Hosea 14:3 – For in You the fatherless find mercy.

Romans 8:29 – For whom He foreknew, He also predestined to be conformed to the image of His Son, that He might be the firstborn among many brethren.

2 Thessalonians 2:13 – But we are bound to give thanks to God always for you, brethren beloved by the Lord, because God from the beginning chose you for salvation through sanctification by the Spirit and belief in the truth.

1 John 3:1 – Behold what manner of love the Father has bestowed on us, that we should be called children of God!

CONTENTMENT

Philippians 4:11-13 - Not that I speak in regard to need, for I have learned in whatever state I am, to be content: I know how to be abased, and I know how to abound. Everywhere and in all things I have learned both to be full and to be hungry, both to abound and to suffer need. I can do all things through Christ who strengthens me.

1 Timothy 6:6 – Now godliness with contentment is great gain.

Hebrews 13:5 – Let your conduct be without covetousness; be content with such things as you have. For He Himself has said, "I will never leave you nor forsake you."

FAITH/TRUSTING THE LORD

Psalm 9:10 – And those who know Your name will put their trust in You; for You, LORD, have not forsaken those who seek You.

Proverbs 3:5-6 – Trust in the LORD with all your heart, and lean not on your own understanding; in all your ways acknowledge Him, and He shall direct your paths.

2 Corinthians 5:7 – For we walk by faith, not by sight.

Hebrews 11:1 – Now faith is the substance of things hoped for, the evidence of things not seen.

Hebrews 11:6 – But without faith it is impossible to please Him, for he who comes to God must believe that He is, and that He is a rewarder of those who diligently seek Him.

FORGIVENESS

Psalm 32:1 – Blessed is he whose transgression is forgiven, whose sin is covered.

Psalm 86:5 – For You, Lord, are good, and ready to forgive, and abundant in mercy to all those who call upon You.

Matthew 6:14 – For if you forgive men their trespasses, your heavenly Father will also forgive you. But if you do not forgive men their trespasses, neither will your Father forgive your trespasses.

Ephesians 4:32 – And be kind to one another, tenderhearted, forgiving one another, even as God in Christ forgave you.

GOD'S SOVEREIGNTY

Genesis 50:20 – But as for you, you meant evil against me; but God meant it for good, in order to bring it about as it is this day, to save many people alive.

Jeremiah 29:11 – For I know the thoughts that I think toward you, says the LORD, thoughts of peace and not evil, to give you a future and a hope.

Romans 8:28 – And we know that all things work together for good to those who love God, to those who are the called according to His purpose.

Romans 12:2– And do not be conformed to this world, but be transformed by the renewing of your mind, that you may prove what is that good and acceptable and perfect will of God.

GREED

Proverbs 1:19 – So are the ways of everyone who is greedy for gain; it takes away the life of its owners.

1 Timothy 6:9-10 – But those who desire to be rich fall into temptation and a snare, and into many foolish and harmful lusts which drown men in destruction and perdition. For the love of money is a root of all kinds of evil, for which some have strayed from the faith in their greediness, and pierced themselves through with many sorrows.

PEACE AND JOY

Psalm 35:9– And my soul shall be joyful in the LORD; it shall rejoice in His salvation.

Isaiah 9:6 - …And His name will be called Wonderful, Counselor, Mighty God, Everlasting Father, Prince of Peace.

Romans 14:17 – for the kingdom of God is not eating and drinking, but righteousness and peace and joy in the Holy Spirit.

Romans 15:13 – Now may the God of hope fill you with all joy and peace in believing, that you may abound in hope by the power of the Holy Spirit.

Galatians 5:22-23– But the fruit of the Spirit is love, joy, peace, longsuffering, kindness, goodness, faithfulness, gentleness, and self-control. Against such there is no law.

1 Peter 1:8-9– Though now you do not see Him, yet believing, you rejoice with joy inexpressible and full of glory, receiving the end of your faith—the salvation of your souls.

PRAYER

Proverbs 15:29– The LORD is far from the wicked, but He hears the prayer of the righteous.

Philippians 4:6-7– Be anxious for nothing, but in everything by prayer and supplication, with thanksgiving, let your requests be made known to God; and the peace of God, which surpasses all understanding, will guard your hearts and minds through Christ Jesus.

Colossians 4:2– Continue earnestly in prayer, being vigilant in it with thanksgiving.

REVENGE/BITTERNESS

Leviticus 19:18– You shall not take vengeance, nor bear any grudge against the children of your people, but you shall love your neighbor as yourself: I am the LORD.

Romans 12:19– Beloved, do not avenge yourselves, but rather give place to wrath; for it is written, "Vengeance is Mine, I will repay," says the Lord.

Hebrews 12:14-15 – Pursue peace with all people, and holiness, without which no one will see the Lord: looking carefully lest anyone fall short of the grace of God; lest any root of bitterness springing up cause trouble, and by this many become defiled.

SIN/SALVATION

Romans 3:23 – for all have sinned and fall short of the glory of God.

Romans 5:18-19 – Therefore, as through one man's offense judgment came to all men, resulting in condemnation, even so through one Man's righteous act the free gift came to all men, resulting in justification of life. For as by one man's disobedience many were made sinners, so also by one Man's obedience many will be made righteous.

Romans 6:23 – For the wages of sin is death, but the gift of God is eternal life in Christ Jesus our Lord.

Romans 10:9 – that if you confess with your mouth the Lord Jesus and believe in your heart that God raised Him from the dead, you will be saved.

THANKFULNESS

Psalm 95:2 – Let us come before His presence with thanksgiving; let us shout joyfully to Him with psalms.

Psalm 100:4 – Enter into His gates with thanksgiving, and into His courts with praise. Be thankful to Him, and bless His name.

Psalm 136:1 – Oh, give thanks to the LORD, for He is good! For His mercy endures forever.

Colossians 3:17 – And whatever you do in word or deed, do all in the name of the Lord Jesus, giving thanks to God the Father through Him.

1 Thessalonians 5:18 – in everything give thanks; for this is the will of God in Christ Jesus for you.